SLEEP WITH STRANGERS

DOLORES HITCHENS

SLEEP WITH STRANGERS

WITH A FOREWORD BY
STEPH CHA

LIBRARY OF AMERICA

SLEEP WITH STRANGERS BY DOLORES HITCHENS
Foreword copyright © 2021 by Literary Classics of the
United States, Inc., New York, N.Y. All rights reserved.

Copyright © 1955 by Dolores Hitchens, renewed 1983
by Patricia Hitchens Johnson and Michael J. Hitchens.
Published by arrangement with the Estate of Dolores Hitchens.

Published by the Library of America.
Visit our website at www.loa.org.

Cover and text design by Donna G. Brown.
Composition by Dianna Logan.

Distributed to the trade in the United States by
Penguin Random House Inc. and in Canada by
Penguin Random House Canada Ltd.

Library of Congress Control Number: 2020952007

ISBN 978-1-59853-697-3

1 3 5 7 9 10 8 6 4 2

Printed in the United States of America

CONTENTS

Foreword by Steph Cha   xi

Sleep with Strangers   1

About Dolores Hitchens and Steph Cha   249

FOREWORD

The woman born Julia Clara Catherine Maria Dolores Robins wrote dozens of novels under four names: the pseudonyms D. B. Olsen, Dolan Birkley, Noel Burke, and, of course, her second married name, Dolores Hitchens. She was a prolific writer with the kind of range that might necessitate multiple pen names, traipsing around the genre with agility and bravado throughout a career that spanned decades–from the 1938 publication of *The Clue in the Clay* to her death in 1973. Her Rachel Murdock series, which featured a spinster detective with a feline sidekick, was an early example of the cat mystery subgenre, now firmly associated with cozy mysteries. Her two James Sader books, *Sleep with Strangers* (1955) and *Sleep with Slander* (1960), lie at the opposite end of the crime spectrum. They are moody, chewy, hard-boiled detective novels with a male private investigator protagonist.

Hitchens was not remarkable because she was a woman, but it would be willful and silly to discuss her legacy, and these novels in particular, without taking her gender into account. Even now, almost fifty years after Hitchens's death, gender and genre remain stubbornly intertwined in crime fiction. Cozy mysteries are written, for the most part, by and for women and ignored or dismissed by male readers and critics to a proportionate degree. Meanwhile, private eye fiction is dominated by men and male archetypes, so much so that female authors in this subgenre are often defined by our difference—our work seen, if not as masculine, as explicitly counter-masculine. It is unsurprising that Bill Pronzini, in praising *Sleep with Slander*, described it as "the best traditional male private eye novel written by a woman" before adding, "and one of the best written by anybody." Pronzini won the Private Eye Writers of America's inaugural Shamus Award for Best P.I. Hardcover Novel in 1982. Only seven female writers have won this award (for a total of ten wins—three for Sue Grafton and two for S. J. Rozan).

There is certainly something traditional about James Sader—he's a sleuth with a moral compass that doesn't depend on law, and he deals with both femmes fatale and alcoholism. Like Philip Marlowe and Lew Archer, he roams around Southern California, burning through shoe leather and pissing people off. His domain is Long Beach, "the town that had grown up from a village by the sea, a city with a hill in the middle of it, sprouting oil derricks like a forest of pins."

We meet Sader in *Sleep with Strangers*, when he visits his new client, Kay Wanderley, "a slender, well-shaped girl with blonde hair." We see him after we see her: "The man on the step was in the act of lighting a cigarette. Rain lay in his hair, which was hatless, and which also, though obviously once reddish, now had faded to a tawny rust laced with gray. He had a lean, sharp, intelligent face. The hands that cupped the match wore a look of mobile strength."

As he tells another woman, "Detectives aren't half as glamorous in real life as they are on TV, or in the movies," and this is true of Sader, who fumbles through both novels without the benefit of any special charisma or genius. What he does have are the plain, well-worn tools of integrity and tenacity, scuffed by age and alcoholism. Unlike the typical boozed-up private eye, Sader is, for the most part, a sober drunk. "I'm a high-dive drinker," he explains. "That first taste of alcohol is the same as jumping off a ten-story building. I'd like to get back up, but I can't." While his relationship with alcohol never takes over the story—no destructive benders, no Alcoholics Anonymous —it's a thread that runs through both novels, taut and threatening as a tripwire. Our man is, at baseline, in a constant struggle for control, and he spends all his time running down liars, cheaters, and killers.

In *Sleep with Strangers*, Sader grapples with a sordid, depressing case about money and corruption that directly recalls Raymond Chandler's *The Big Sleep*. There's a rich old man, a few young, wayward women—even a pivotal oil sump. But while his streets are just as mean, Sader is a shabbier hero than Marlowe:

He'd been young once, yes; but that was over. It was really and finally over. The bitter truth was that he was now a tired man with gray in his hair, with the beginning of a stoop, and no amount of frenzy or cunning, no wishing . . . could bring back that which had gone forever. There must be a time like this in everyone's life, he thought numbly. When all your illusions go down the drain. When you see at last what you have lost.

Sader develops an infatuation with Kay, and in one of the novel's wackier episodes, he more or less abducts her, taking her to Vegas to hide away and possibly marry, against her will and for what he mistakenly believes is her own good. Marlowe—who threw a young, willing, naked Carmen Sternwood out of his bed—would never have acted so desperate.

But Sader's flaws and foibles make him a compelling character, worth following as he wanders around Long Beach looking for answers, digging until he hits the truth. He solves the case, but there's more to it than that. His investigation leads him to a forceful confrontation with reality, as well as the pain of adapting to that reality. Kay Wanderley offers a similar theory about her missing mother: "She had a world that she loved and it fell apart, and then she was lost. She was like a child alone in the dark."

Sleep with Slander is more or less literally about a child alone in the dark. Sader is hired by Hale Gibbings, a wealthy sixty-year-old architect, who tells him, "I need most of all an honest man. Yes . . . a kind of crook, and yet honest." Gibbings asks him to track down a five-year-old boy being abused by an unknown party in an unknown place. Sader doesn't trust his client and his task proves remarkably frustrating, with even the most basic facts about the child and his origins proving difficult to pin down.

There was something inside the amorphous case, a hard core he couldn't quite get a grip on. He tried to think of a comparison and remembered something his grandmother had said once, something about a flatiron inside a feather bed. There was a flatiron somewhere inside this thing but he couldn't find it. He just knew that it was there. A booby trap.

The case twists and plunges admirably, and through it all, Sader holds on, propelled by a simple core of decency and the fact of this suffering child: "You couldn't endure thinking of the child's body subjected to abuse; the tears were warm and wet, and the sobs were something you heard if you stopped to listen." Pronzini was right: *Sleep with Slander* should be a classic of the private investigator genre. It has the breadth and the depth, the memorable characters, the vivid style, and the brutal emotional impact of the best hard-boiled detective fiction.

Of course, Hitchens had some of the blind spots you might expect of a white American writer of her era. Almost all of the characters in these books are white, and when they're not, the difference is very much noted. A "chocolate-colored maid" appears and disappears within a sentence; a half-Asian supporting character in *Sleep with*

Strangers has a larger part, but every time she shows up, we hear about her "exotic, oriental eyes." To be fair, Long Beach was, as of the 1950 census, 97.4 percent white. These days, it's a majority minority city that's given us Snoop Dogg and a vibrant Cambodia Town, the largest ethnically Cambodian community outside of Cambodia. It also has a new literary sleuth: Joe Ide's Isaiah Quintabe, a brilliant Black detective in the Sherlock Holmes tradition, presiding over the bustling life of contemporary Long Beach.

But Ide's work doesn't overwrite Hitchens's any more than mine overwrites Chandler's. *Sleep with Strangers* and *Sleep with Slander* capture a different era of Long Beach's history, and Sader is the perfect guide—a dogged private investigator who muddles through darkness, "realizing that the city in which he had grown up had a side to it he had never known," and shining light wherever he goes.

Steph Cha
Los Angeles, November 2020

SLEEP WITH STRANGERS

CHAPTER ONE

At about two o'clock in the afternoon the rain began to blow in from the sea. It moved at first on irregular gusts, whistling hit-and-run spatters that promised the downpour to come. Woolen clouds rolled through the sky, and the sea was slate-colored. Below the bluff, the noise of the surf made a continuous thunder. The rain burst at last upon the terrace of the big house in Scotland Place and inside, by the glass doors, the girl who stood watching frowned and drew back. She was a slender, well-shaped girl with blonde hair pinned up high, dressed in a dark blue suit, red shoes, and a lot of rhinestone jewelry. Her expression was anxious and trouble lay deep in the big gray eyes. Her worries seemed to concern the furniture on the terrace. All the gay cushions were getting wet.

On a covered swing lay what appeared to be a roll of bedding, tucked up into an army blanket of khaki wool. The girl's gaze was searching and restless on this bundle, flitting back and forth over it as if inwardly she were tormented by a desire to rescue it from the rain. She put out a hand suddenly, perhaps for the door handle; but at this instant a bell buzzed in some other part of the house. She jerked her hand back, rubbed it for a moment, then turned quickly, crossed the room, and entered the hall. At its other end was a big door, flanked by greenery and topped by a fanlight. She paused in the hall, examining its gloom; and then before opening the door she clicked a wall switch, illuminating the chandelier in the ceiling.

The man on the step was in the act of lighting a cigarette. Rain lay in his hair, which was hatless, and which also, though obviously once reddish, now had faded to a tawny rust laced with gray. He had a lean, sharp, intelligent face. The hands that cupped the match wore a look of mobile strength. He was tall; his height was lessened by his being somewhat stooped. The girl met his gaze without speaking. Her attitude was watchful and reserved.

He dropped the packet of matches into a pocket of his belted raincoat. He took the cigarette from his mouth. "You're Miss Wanderley? I'm Sader. You called me a little while ago." His eyes went all over her in one swift summing up.

She stepped back into the hall. "Yes. Come in, please."

She led the way back into the big room that joined the terrace and there paused as if uncertain about what to say. She stood twisting a finger in the loop of her belt. Sader pulled back the raincoat and fished a wallet from the hip pocket of his suit. He showed her his private operator's license and other identification. "You don't know me. I could be anybody."

"Oh, I didn't doubt who you were. You were recommended to me—"

"By whom?"

"A—a friend. Since I was quite determined—" Apparently she decided not to finish this. Perhaps she felt she had ventured too quickly upon the business between them. She spent a moment thinking, the gray eyes studying the buttons of Sader's raincoat.

He gave her time to make up her mind. He went over to the plate-glass doors and looked out at the roiling storm. "Overdue," he commented.

"Yes. It's been dry too long." She sounded as if her throat were suffering a drought, too. Her tone was scratchy, nervous.

He waited a little longer and then prodded her. "Can't you tell me what kind of job it is?" She answered with an uncomprehending stare, so he went on: "Do you want somebody followed? Or does someone owe you money? Or could it be dirty and dramatic like blackmail?"

She roused, shook her head. "It isn't any of those things, Mr. Sader. I want you to find my mother. She's missing." As Sader left the door she hurried over to it, pulled the draperies—stiff peach-colored brocade—not quite shut; and through the space left open she peered fleetingly at the furniture on the terrace.

Sader took a chair; she came to sit opposite. The furniture was nice. Sader decided that it had cost money, quite a lot of money, about eight or nine years ago and had had good care since. There was a mahogany grand in one corner, polished like a mirror. The couch the girl sat on was a good deal bigger than the one at home in his apartment. About eighteen feet long, he thought. Foam rubber hadn't been used yet when it was built, so the springs must be good. It looked nearly new. It was finished in rose velvet, and the girl made a pretty and harmonious picture except for the red leather pumps. They clashed with the rose velvet.

"How long has your mother been gone?"

"She left the house three nights ago—Tuesday—at about eleven o'clock. I haven't seen or heard from her since."

"You've made inquiries?"

"Oh, yes. All the usual things. Her friends. Hospitals."

"Jail?"

She smiled thinly as if he had made a poor joke but should be rewarded a little for effort. "Yes, I even tried that."

"You reported her absence to the police?"

"No. I don't think Mother would want it handled that way."

"They're your best bet," Sader advised. She shook her head. He said, "Well, how about an ad in the newspaper?"

"Are you trying to tell me you don't want the job, Mr. Sader?"

It was his turn to smile. He took a last pull on the cigarette and crushed it out in an onyx ashtray on a table by his elbow. "Tell me about her. Name, age, marital status. Who her friends are. What she likes for amusement." He stretched his feet on the Persian carpet.

The girl looked at his feet as if she thought he shouldn't relax quite that much, at first. He sensed that she wanted him to be as stirred up and worried as she was about her mother's being gone. She said, "Her name is Felicia

Wanderley and she's forty-seven. Dad died seven years ago and Mother never remarried. She's lived in Long Beach all her life. As for amusements, well, she has a few old friends she's known for ages. Some of them give bridge parties, and they go to shows." A quiver ran over the girl's frame and Sader guessed how she held herself under rigid control. She was fearful, or embarrassed, or mystified; or perhaps a mixture of all of these feelings boiled in her mind.

"What about romantic attachments?" Sader asked.

"Mother's?" She waited for him to correct his impertinence and when he didn't she reproved him with: "Mother hasn't had a man friend for years."

"That you know of," he put in gently.

She was going to be stubborn about this. The gray eyes were stony. "No, you mustn't expect to find anything along that line. Mother had long ago lost interest in men. I don't mean she was narrow-minded, a prude. She liked fun. But it was all platonic."

Sader's mouth took on a quirk. "How old are you?"

A quick color bloomed in her cheeks. "I'm twenty-two. I know what you're thinking, that I'm like one of these stupid teen-agers, that I think middle-aged love is nasty. You're wrong. I'd have liked it very much if Mother had met and fallen in love with a suitable man her age. It would have been normal and pleasant. Let's not get confused. Mother hasn't eloped. She wouldn't, anyway, without telling me."

"Very well," Sader said, as if chastened. "Where do you think she is?"

Fright leaped in her eyes. "I don't know. That's why I called you."

They looked at each other across the space between Sader's chair and her rose velvet couch. The rhinestone earrings she wore glittered in the cloudy light let in by the windows. Between the earrings was a face that interested Sader; it had character as well as beauty—quite a bit of character for a girl just twenty-two. Her makeup had been applied lightly and skillfully. Sader took a small dog-eared notebook and a pen from his coat. He leafed through the book to a blank page. "Where were you when she left the house?"

"I was in my bathroom doing some stockings," the girl answered. "Mother rapped at the door, and when I answered, she peeped in. She said she'd called a cab and was going out for a short while, but that I wasn't to worry if she happened to be late."

Sader asked, "What was she wearing?"

"A white blouse, silk, with pleats down the front. Green slacks. A beaver coat. It's a very nice coat. She carried a big brown handbag."

"How much money in it?"

"I don't know."

"Anything on her head?"

"She had a green scarf wound to keep her hair back."

Sader tapped the notebook with the blunt end of the pen and looked at Miss Wanderley. "Did she give you any hint of where she was going?" When the girl shook her head, he said, "Was that the usual thing?"

She hesitated. "She nearly always told me where she meant to go. And yet I didn't think too much about it, then. I didn't worry. One of Mother's cronies keeps pretty late

8

hours. Sometimes she calls Mother to meet her some-where, some bar or other. I thought that may have hap-pened Tuesday night."

"And did it?"

"No. Tina Griffin says she didn't meet Mother."

"Does your mother drink quite a bit?"

"Not too much." Miss Wanderley's expression showed her distaste for the query, perhaps for Sader's presuming to ask it. Then she decided to add to her answer. "I suppose most people, if they drink at all, drink more as they get older."

"I suppose most of us do," he agreed. He noted that she controlled the sharp glance she must have wanted to give him. He examined the room again. "How does your mother make her living?"

"She dabbles some in real estate. It's just a sideline with her. Dad left property that supports us."

Sader sat quietly for a couple of minutes. "Does your mother keep any record of appointments?"

"Yes, but in a haphazard fashion. I'll get her desk memo." She rose and hurried from the room and was gone for sev-eral minutes. During this time Sader strolled over to the glass door and looked out. He put away the pen and note-book and lit a cigarette. Outdoors, big drops were pelting the glass and wending their way downward in twiggy pat-terns, and beyond, the flagstone terrace with its gay swing and the awning-covered lounges looked like a circus lost in the rain. A corner of the army blanket which covered the roll of stuff in the swing had worked loose, and under it showed a scrap of something else that looked like wet fur.

Sader studied it thoughtfully. Then he heard Miss Wanderley's returning steps and turned around.

She stopped just inside the door as if his position surprised her. "Is something wrong?"

"Just taking a stretch." He went back to the couch and she met him there. She carried a large photograph in a silver frame and a leather-bound desk pad. She handed him the picture.

"It was taken last year. It's a very good likeness."

He'd seen the picture before; its familiarity teased him.

"Mother never has looked her age," the girl continued. "She's small and slender. There's no trace of gray in her hair. Most people think she's in her thirties."

"Until they meet you."

She smiled fleetingly. "Yes. Until . . . and if . . . they meet me."

He looked at her over the cigarette. She and her mother did not much resemble each other. There was something solid behind the girl's prettiness, some quality of common sense or directness that he could sense; but the woman in the picture was like a fluffy bird. The small face was tipped up to meet the camera, perhaps also to give a flattering neckline. The soft hair curled and clung about the mother's throat. It was the expression of the mouth he instantly disliked. Bee-stung, he thought; that's what they used to call it. Actresses pouted like that in the twenties.

He gave her the framed picture. "If you have one, I'd prefer a snapshot. To take with me."

She nodded. "Yes, I'll get one." She handed him the memo pad.

He sat down to leaf through it. As she had said, the entries were scattered and, to him, mostly meaningless. On Monday Mrs. Wanderley had written:

> *Beauty Shop 10:30*
> *(Try the henna?)*
> *See the man, house on Plenty Street*
> *Phone 201–111*
> *Margot's, drinks, 5*

He turned the sheet to Tuesday.

> *License for Tootsie*
> *Get refund on car . . . $65, no less*
> *Cleaner's*
> *Charlie Ott, Plenty Street, 3:15*

The girl was bending over the back of his chair. He flipped the pages. "I judge you've studied these."

"Yes. This Mr. Ott has a duplex he wants Mother to sell for him. Margot is one of her old friends. She has a home on Signal Hill. I called her today and she said Mother was there Monday, late in the afternoon, and didn't stay too long."

"Have you phoned Mr. Ott?"

"I tried. I haven't found him in yet." Worry underscored each word.

"Who's Tootsie?"

The girl drew a sharp breath. "Our little dog. On Tuesday Mother got a new license for her, about eleven according to the man at the pound. The item about her car concerns an argument she's having with the garage over some repairs. They say she came in around noon, talked to the service manager, didn't settle anything, and left. That's the last definite check I've been able to make."

Sader closed the desk memo, put it down, and took out his own notebook and did some scribbling. "I want names and addresses, your mother's friends."

She hesitated, and then out of sight behind him, she spoke in a rush. "Before you start, shouldn't we discuss your fee, or wages?"

Sader didn't turn to look at her. "It's thirty-five a day, plus expenses." To himself he thought, that's going to stop her. She'll tell me she'll think it over and let me know. This house and everything in it speaks of a careful management of money—except that stuff getting drowned on the terrace.

But she said, "That's all right. Do you want an advance?"

"No. I'll send a bill when I'm finished."

"When you've found Mother, you mean?"

Now Sader looked back at her. "When I can tell you where she is."

She smiled the brief, disconcerted smile. "You mean—if she's run off and won't see anyone, but you trace her somehow. Is that it?"

"Am I right in thinking that you want to know whether your mother is alive and well and operating under her own power and volition? That she isn't in trouble, or suffering from amnesia?"

The gray eyes were cloudy with torment. "I guess that sums it up."

"I can't drag her back if she doesn't want to come. People walk out on their old lives all the time. When they're through, they're through."

"There isn't any romance." The girl's tone was definite, dismissing any question. "I'll trust you to do whatever needs to be done."

Sader handed her the notebook. "Give me the names of her friends and where I can find them. And then get me a snapshot."

"Yes, sir," she said primly, and sat down to write.

Sader climbed the stairs and walked down the hall to his office. The light was gray. The clouds had settled low over the city. He pushed in through the door; the small outer room was empty. In the inner office his partner, Dan Scarborough, was waiting for him.

Dan was younger than Sader, taller, heavier. He dressed carefully. He had a stocky frame, a shock of black hair, and the expression on his good-looking face was usually eager and helpful, what Sader called his St. Bernard's look. He said, "Hi. Had lunch?"

"I took a call. I guess I forgot lunch. What about the job for Ajoukian?"

"I saw the old man," said Dan. "The son has been missing since Tuesday. He went out in the evening for a few drinks, and maybe a little business afterward, and didn't come home again. From what I could get out of the old man, his business now is buying and selling oil shares. He's a close-mouthed old bugger where money lies. I met the son's wife, too. Anybody who'd walk out on a dish like that ought to have his head examined. Here's a couple of sandwiches." He opened a drawer of his desk and took out a brown paper sack.

The two desks sat back to back. They were steel desks, painted olive green. The rug was oatmeal-colored. The only other furniture in the room besides the two desks and their matching chairs was a red leather lounge under the windows. Sader threw his raincoat on the lounge and went over to Dan's desk and examined the inside of the paper sack. "This time it's peanut butter?"

"Sardines," said Dan virtuously. "Don't you know it's Friday?"

"I'm astonished that you remembered it," Sader said. He took out a sardine sandwich and sat on the corner of Dan's desk to eat it. "I've got a job, too. A disappearance. A woman named Felicia Wanderley dropped from sight on Tuesday night. Her daughter wants her back."

"Lots of people going away from Long Beach," said Dan thoughtfully. "And it's not such a big town, as towns go. Both skipping out on Tuesday—could there be a connection?"

Sader was looking at the window, where rain hung on the glass like a pattern in sequins. "We've both lived in Long Beach so long, we think of it as it used to be. The way it was before the war. A village, you might say. The town's grown up. If the Wanderley woman knew Ajoukian, it would be a miracle."

"It would save time if they were together," Dan suggested, munching sardines.

"The Wanderleys are old, Iowa-style society," Sader said. "Pioneers, financed by mortgages. I know the type, I grew up in this town. They used to own all the big homes along Ocean Avenue, and they were acquainted only with each other."

"Like the Cabots and God?"

"Now they're smothered in Long Beach's new rich, the café owners, the car-agency millionaires, the oil crowd."

"The oil crowd isn't new," Dan corrected. "They swooped in here in the twenties."

"The oil crowd is new compared to people like the Wanderleys. And what is Ajoukian?"

"Now you sound like a goddam snob," Dan said.

"I mean, what is Ajoukian if you were Mrs. Wanderley?"

"From his picture, I'd say that to any dame under ninety, Ajoukian was hell on wheels. It's just my opinion," Dan answered, licking his fingers.

CHAPTER TWO

"Ajoukian, Sr., must be over sixty. White hair. Lots of wrinkles. Shakes a bit. He's really excited about his son's disappearance. The wife—well, that blonde fluffy kind, they've always got something like a manicure on their minds." Dan sighed.

"The wife's good-looking?"

Dan puckered up and whistled in reply, a tribute to the many perfections of Mrs. Ajoukian. "I could describe her in detail, but you might think I wasn't a gentleman," he summed up. "As for Ajoukian, Jr.: the old man showed me a photo. Junior's dark, very masculine, sulky. I didn't take in too much at first until I saw the sly attention the old man was giving me. Then I did a double take. He expected me not to like the guy, his own son, and he was enjoying that expectation. Ajoukian the younger has what Valentino used to have. You name it. And before you say anything, Papa, may I remind you I don't remember Mr. Valentino except from seeing the old films on TV." He smirked wisely at his partner. "I would say that the young Ajoukian looks dangerous in a sexual manner. He might leap at a girl out of dark corners, even if he was married to her, just for kicks."

Sader smiled faintly. "What kind of place do they have?"

"Oh, big and rustic. You know what they're doing now out in Garden Grove. Ranches, all ranches. Farmhouse, barn, stalls, split-rail fences, pasture, duckpond, orange grove, walnuts—and all on one and a half acres. The Ajoukians are pretty used to it; they show no signs of having lived for twenty years on the Hill behind Father Ajoukian's junk tool yard. Mama Ajoukian died a few years back, as I remember. I guess that must have been the signal to move. She probably spoke with a thicker Syrian accent than Father's. Be agony, dragging her to cocktail parties in that neck of the woods."

"They'll have no trouble standing the tariff," Sader said.

"No, and Father Ajoukian even offered a bonus if we find the son within three days."

"When did Ajoukian start buying oil shares?"

"Don't know. He didn't say. He was so very, very cautious about giving away any business secrets, I couldn't help wondering if part of the technique was robbing widows and orphans. He muttered something about having an eye on an old well that wasn't doing too much but might produce better if it were rebored, or whatever they do to oil wells. Young Ajoukian went out at eight o'clock Tuesday night. He just never came home again."

"What's your best lead?" Sader asked.

"The Hill, of course," said Dan. "And brother, do I hate the stink of oil and gas and that boozy steam they have coming out of pipes all over." He looked into the paper sack and saw it was empty. "Do you think I could kill that fish flavor with a shot of rum?"

"The fish won't care." Sader had finished his own sandwich. He went out into the anteroom where the water cooler stood in a corner with a rack of paper cups. He drank two cups of water and came back to the inner office. "Did Ajoukian's father give you a picture?"

"Didn't have one to spare. But look, the Ajoukians, father and son, have been on the Hill in one way or another for umpteen years. Everybody knows them, I shouldn't have any trouble running down anybody who saw him Tuesday night."

"That's right."

"What're you going to do to begin on this Wanderley woman?"

"The taxi," Sader said. "She's supposed to have taken a cab from home."

But within thirty-five minutes Sader knew that no woman had ordered a cab late Tuesday night from Scotland Place.

It was a point he decided to clarify at once, since Miss Wanderley's mention of the cab had been casual. He telephoned her. She came on the wire with a breathless murmur. "Hello? Kay Wanderley speaking."

"This is Sader again. I've been trying to run down the driver of the cab your mother took Tuesday night. I can't find him."

"Oh, I should have told you," she said, still breathless. "A friend—this same friend who recommended you"—(Who in hell is he, Sader wondered?)—"knows an official in one of the taxi firms here. He checked for us, his company and the others, and couldn't find any record of her call. He said there were two possibilities."

"She didn't take a cab," Sader said. "Or she just hailed one passing by, and he happened to be knocking down on the company."

"Yes, that's what the conclusion was."

"I wanted to be sure I'd heard you right," Sader said. "She did tell you she'd called a taxi?"

"I—I'm pretty sure that's what she said."

"She couldn't have said, 'I'm going to get a taxi'?"

There was silence on the other end of the wire. Then Kay Wanderley made up her mind. "I don't think so."

"I'd like your permission to offer a reward to any driver who can give us information," Sader told her. "Not using your mother's name, of course. Just a description. There won't be any clue to your mother's identity."

"It's okay," she answered, the first slang he'd heard her use.

She hadn't asked how big the reward should be, but Sader told her he thought it should be at least fifty dollars. That sum should smoke out something if there was anything to get. Even a driver who was cheating his company would be tempted to contact Sader privately.

She listened and agreed. Then Sader added: "Is there anything else I ought to know? Anything else you've done already on your own? Or anything"—he searched for a phrase—"anything that's frightened you?"

There was a long silence then, and during the time Sader wondered, as he had on first hearing the girl's story, why she had waited three days past her mother's disappearance to ask help on it. Most daughters in similar straits, he thought, would have rushed down to the police that first morning. Of course, there had been the help offered by the mysterious friend of whom Miss Wanderley had spoken, the friend who seemed to know Sader enough to recommend him for the job of finding Mama. Sader speculated as to whether the friend might be someone he'd known in the Army. Then the girl's voice crackled on the wire.

"I'll call you if I think of anything further," she said with the touch of primness he remembered.

"Good-bye, then," said Sader.

"Good-bye."

I'd like to talk to your friend, he thought, looking at the phone and imagining Miss Wanderley still listening. Was he the one who cautioned you against publicity? Did he remind you of some failing, some escapade, which might explain Mama's running away? And if Mother Wanderley didn't have any romantic notions, do you? And is he it?

The office was empty, Dan having made his departure after downing the shot of rum. Sader dropped the dog-eared notebook on the desk and leafed through it to the pages of scribbling about Mrs. Wanderley. He found the telephone number, 201–111, dialed it. A man's voice came on. "Hello."

"Mr. Ott?"

"That's right." Mr. Ott's tone was growling, impatient. He was in a hurry, or he had things on his mind. He didn't sound as if he had much information to give over the telephone.

Sader said, "I'm selling insurance, Mr. Ott. We've got a splendid new policy for people like you."

"People like me don't need insurance," Mr. Ott growled, and hung up.

"You interest me," Sader said into the dead phone, "and for that I shall give you some personal attention. As soon as I spread the word about Miss Wanderley's fifty dollar reward." He slapped the book shut and stuck it into his pocket, and left the office, making sure that the hall door was securely locked. There were no records, no money, but there was Dan's rum. He was fond of it; he wouldn't want it stolen.

Mr. Ott's duplex dwelling was located on an east-west street above the traffic of Highway 101, which crosses Long Beach just below the fringe of Signal Hill. His house faced north and must on sunny days give a view of the heights of the Hill, its pin-cushion tangle of derricks, tanks, and the towers of refineries. Sader parked a half block from the place, after passing it once. Rain washed down his windshield in a steady torrent, was only momentarily swept aside by the wipers. Judging by what he could see through the wet glass, Mr. Ott's duplex was an up-and-down affair, and somewhat better built and kept than the rest of the neighborhood. The lower half was finished in white pine siding, the upper in blue stucco. The ornamental shutters were stone-gray, the porch steps painted red. Sader decided that Mr. Ott was perhaps a painter, or perhaps had spruced up the place for Mrs. Wanderley to sell it.

He left the car without locking it, walked quickly

through the downpour to Mr. Ott's front porch. He rang the bell and waited.

Shuffling steps sounded inside, the door drew open, and a giant of a man looked out at him through the screen. He had an immense tangle of fuzzy gray hair, about two days' growth of whiskers, and underwear which buttoned up the front—if there had been buttons. Right now it was pinned up the front, and the pants below had the suspenders hanging, as if Mr. Ott had been about to put on a shirt, or to shave.

Sader said politely, "I'm sorry to disturb you, Mr. Ott, but I'm making inquiries about a friend of yours who has disappeared. May I talk to you?"

Ott's glance congealed with what Sader took for enmity. "You mean Felicia Wanderley? Nuh, I don't know where she is."

"You had heard that she disappeared?"

"Margot Cole told me. She said Felicia's girl had been telephoning everybody."

Sader touched the handle of the screen door tentatively. "Do you mind if I come in?"

Ott drew back grudgingly, and Sader took this as an invitation to open the screen and follow him into the house. They passed down a short hall and into Mr. Ott's living room. The house needed the touch of a broom in about the same degree as Mr. Ott needed the application of a razor. The furnishings weren't worn or shabby, though there was a lack of taste, harmony; and right now everything was quite dusty. Nothing here resembled the glossy, settled luxury of the Wanderley home, and this caused Sader to wonder about the acquaintance between Mrs. Wanderley and Ott.

Ott sat down on the edge of a chair, gingerly, as if Sader's presence made him ill at ease. Sader said, "Did you see Mrs. Wanderley on Tuesday?"

"She was here for ten or fifteen minutes, waiting for a buyer to show up. He didn't come and she decided he hadn't been serious."

In the moment of silence following, above the wash of rain at the windows, Sader heard a whistle on the Hill, a high hoarse blast; and he wondered how Dan was getting along up there, asking after young Ajoukian. "Was there anything unusual about Mrs. Wanderley? In her manner. In what she said."

"Not a thing." Ott supported his paunch by folding his hands under it. "She got sore about the guy not coming around after he'd said he would. That's all."

"What was his name?"

"She didn't tell me. You know how real-estate people are. They try to be so damned mysterious. Afraid you and the buyer might get together without them." He sucked his front teeth loudly.

"How was she dressed?"

Ott looked disgusted. "How would I know? She had on clothes—a dress, I guess, coat, hat, shoes."

"A fur coat?"

"I don't remember. I've got no memory for women's doodads."

Sader took out cigarettes, offered Ott the pack. Ott took a cigarette after a moment's hesitation, then looked it over as if suspecting Sader of some trick. After Sader had lit both cigarettes, he said, "What do you think might have happened to Mrs. Wanderley? Would she have walked out on her home and her daughter?"

Ott's eyes narrowed; he didn't look at Sader but at the burning tip of the cigarette in his hand. "Women," he said, as if this summed it all up.

Sader waited a moment or two, then persisted, "You think she would have?"

"They'll do anything," Ott growled.

"How did you meet her? How long ago?" Sader saw Ott's anger, just under the surface, and added, "I'm not trying to pry into your affairs. I'm on a job, part of the work is asking questions. Don't take it personally."

Ott drew heavily on the cigarette. He moved back a little in the chair. "I met Felicia Wanderley a long time ago. I knew her husband before he died. We drilled a few wells together. What I mean is, I drilled them. He put up the money."

A bell rang in the recesses of Sader's mind. He said, "Do you know a father and son named Ajoukian?"

Ott looked at him through the smoke. "That crumb? Who don't? I been gypped by him plenty when I was on the Hill and had to rustle up some tools in a hurry. Thank God I got out of the oil game." He drew on the cigarette, then added, "I'm talking about the old man. I don't know young Ajoukian."

"Do you think Felicia Wanderley knew these people?"

Ott's fuzzy gray brows climbed toward his hairline. "How would she?"

"Ajoukian's business these last few years isn't selling tools, it's investing in oil shares."

"That still wouldn't bring them together," Ott said. "Wanderley and I drilled, and we sold. It's all gone years ago."

"She has no interest in any oil properties?"

"Nothing I know of," Ott answered slowly. "I don't get the drift, mister. Why are you trying to connect her with the Ajoukians?"

"Young Ajoukian dropped from sight on the day Mrs. Wanderley disappeared, Tuesday."

Ott sat still and silent for a minute. "You're working on that, too?"

"My partner's on the Hill now, asking about Ajoukian."

Ott got up and walked restlessly across the room to the windows. The curtains looked dusty; he pushed them aside and Sader saw the glass, sparkling with water. "The old man made a lot of money," he said finally, without looking at Sader. "He had a shack back of his yard, and kept his old lady there. He'd have sheltered a cow better. What I say about women, it don't apply to Mrs. Ajoukian. She was square and decent and kindhearted. She fed anybody she figured was hungry, providing Ajoukian wasn't there to keep her from giving food away. She whitewashed the inside of the shack, she kept the kids clean—they had a little girl; she died—and my guess is she never had any idea the money Ajoukian made. She was too ignorant to know about banks. Too dumb to know her own rights." He came back to his chair and sat down in it, solidly this time. "We got off Mrs. Wanderley."

"I'm glad you could fill in even a little about the Ajoukians," Sader told him. "I'll pass along what you've told me to my partner. Sometimes the secret of what's happened lies in the background, sometimes a long way back into the past."

"I haven't seen the Ajoukians, father nor son, for years," Ott said quickly. "I heard he'd moved out of town and that his son got married."

"You never heard Mrs. Wanderley mention them?"

"Nuh. Would she know somebody who made money in junk?"

"My partner saw young Ajoukian's picture. He says the boy is handsome."

Ott showed no spark of interest, and Sader wondered if he could be as indifferent as he seemed. "I guess he don't resemble his old man. Look, if this is all you got to ask—"

Sader stood up promptly. "Just one thing more. Did Mrs. Wanderley come here Tuesday in a taxi?"

Ott shook his head. "I don't know. Could be. I didn't see a cab. I had the idea she might have come on the bus."

Sader snapped his fingers in vexation. The big yellow buses were so much a part of Long Beach's congested traffic picture that he'd ignored them. And as clearly as if he were looking at one now, he imagined the yellow behemoth stopping at the corner of Ocean Avenue, opposite the entrance to Scotland Place, and Mrs. Wanderley stepping into the glow of its headlights Tuesday night.

"Her car's laid up," Ott was saying. "She put it in a garage."

"Yes, I know that." Sader moved toward the hall. I'm

so used to driving a car, he thought in self-scorn, I forget that some people still use public transportation. And his thoughts added, if Mrs. Wanderley took a bus from Scotland Place and got off downtown, you'll have one hell of a time tracing her. Unless she asked for a transfer, and the driver remembers.

At the door he offered his hand to Ott and the big man took it, though with a hint of reluctance. Ott's fingers were flabby and warm and a little sticky. He muttered, half embarrassed, "Well, now, I'll go back to my nap."

He hadn't been about to don a shirt, then, nor shave. He'd been in bed. Sader said, "If you hear from Mrs. Wanderley, hear anything about her, will you call her daughter, or me?" He gave Ott his business card.

"Sader and Scarborough," Ott read aloud, slowly. "Sure, I'll call."

Sader went back to his car and drove away. The hope that Mrs. Wanderley had taken a bus on Tuesday night stayed with him until evening, until he had run down and questioned the last driver who might possibly have picked her up in the vicinity of Scotland Place. Then Sader was faced with the truth. It was beginning to look as if Mrs. Wanderley had vanished in the very instant in which she had closed the door of Kay Wanderley's bathroom.

There was some other explanation, of course. Someone in a car had picked her up. A mythical somebody. Yeah, Sader told himself, a wraith.

Among the tangle of other ideas, he played with one which suggested that Mrs. Wanderley might never have left home at all.

CHAPTER THREE

Sader drove back downtown, turned west on Broadway, left the car in a parking lot, and walked to his office just off Pine. It was dark now. The pavements were black and shining under the street lights. In the office he found Dan putting on his overcoat. "Going to eat?"

"Yeah. I've got a treat coming. Mrs. Ajoukian just called. She thinks I ought to come out to their place and let them feed me. She wants to know, do I like lobster? I said yes, if it's thermidor, and since this is Friday."

"You'd say yes anytime." Sader threw down his raincoat and sat down at his desk and ran a hand over his reddish, graying head.

"You look tired, Papa," Dan said solicitously. "How's Mrs. Wanderley coming along? You want her daughter to ask *you* to dinner? I could drop a hint."

Sader leaned back in the chair, took out cigarettes.

"That's another thing. You're smoking yourself to death."

Sader struck a match. "Tell me about young Ajoukian."

"I can't get a lead," Dan complained. "Oh, I don't mean

28

I didn't get information. I went up on the Hill, I talked to guys in field offices, in tool warehouses, on derricks, on top of tanks. They all know young Ajoukian. Nobody seems to dislike him too much."

"And–Tuesday?"

"Some of them thought they might have seen him Tuesday. Nobody was sure."

Sader blew smoke at the olive-green desk top; it fanned there, floated in the air. The rain was a whisper at the window, underlining the quiet of the room. Dan took the bottle from his desk drawer, poured himself a shot of rum, and tossed it off. Sader watched his movements without seeing them. He was reviewing the day. It had begun with the call from Mr. Ajoukian. After the nondescript cases which had filled recent weeks, the Ajoukian affair had roused Sader's interest and promised something more involved than shadowing deadbeats and errant husbands. He was vaguely familiar with the career of Ajoukian, Sr., since the rise of the immigrant had been spectacular enough to invite newspaper comment. Ajoukian was always referred to as an oil-tool tycoon. The yard at the top of the Hill, tucked in among pumping wells, as Sader recalled it, had been full of rusty junk; and he seemed to recall also that more than once the police had been interested in Mr. Ajoukian's sources of supply.

The thought of young Ajoukian walking out on all this had intrigued Sader.

"I ran into a coincidence," he told Dan. Dan paused at the door. Sader continued, "I scratched an old friend of Mrs. Wanderley and uncovered an old enemy of Ajoukian's."

Dan hurried back to the desk. "Hey, you remember what I said this morning? I told you—"

"I said *coincidence*," Sader put in. He went on to tell Dan about Ott, what Ott had said about young Ajoukian's dead mother. "Ott lives just below Signal Hill. He used to drill up there. Of course he'd know Ajoukian. There must be hundreds like him scattered all over Southern California."

Dan drummed his fingers on the desk. "Yeah, but he knows Mrs. Wanderley. There's a connection, Jim. I feel it. I've got a hunch."

"You're hypnotized by Tuesday," Sader said calmly. "When you've been in this racket as long as I have, you'll learn better."

"You sound old, Papa."

Sader got up and went out to the water cooler and got a drink. When he came back, he said, "Run along to dinner. I'm going to phone Miss Wanderley. Then I'm going home." He turned his back to Dan and began to dial Kay Wanderley's number.

He knew she was crying before she said a word. Then he had to listen to her apologies. She didn't want him to think she had expected results so quickly.

"What is it, then?" he asked.

"I—I kept thinking she'd just walk in," Kay Wanderley sobbed. "Any minute, I expected her step in the hall. I listened for her voice. Only now it's raining, a rainy night, and all at once I don't—I don't really expect her any more."

"Yes, I know what you mean. Shall I come out and talk to you?"

Her voice was a whisper. "Please. Would you?"

Dinner postponed, Sader told himself, getting his raincoat.

It turned out that there was a housekeeper, a gray mouse of about fifty with an air of motherly distinction. She took his coat in the hall, surveyed his suit as if resisting an impulse to jerk it off him for cleaning and pressing, and told him Miss Wanderley was waiting for him in the living room. He lit a cigarette before moving on, and she said, "Lovely tobacco!" in a noticeably English accent.

Kay Wanderley was standing at the living-room door. "Annie, we might as well eat at once." She looked at Sader. "That is, if you'll have dinner with us."

"Thanks, I'd appreciate that." Out of Sader's mind drifted the prospect of the cafeteria meal, the steam-washed food, crowded tables.

Annie had turned, but Kay said, "Mrs. Simms, I'd like to present Mr. Sader. He's the private detective who's looking for Mother."

"So happy to meet you." Maybe she meant it. She bustled away like a small busy hen.

Kay led him into the living room. As she walked ahead, he sized up her outfit. She wore a gray dress, a glowing misty silk that reminded him of the color of her eyes. Black pumps. The rhinestones, glittering under the lights. She turned, and he noted the soft hair curling in gauzy feathers over her temples. She was a pretty woman, he thought. Kid, he corrected himself.

The marks of tears had been dusted over with powder, but they were there.

Sader said, "I take it you've talked thoroughly with your housekeeper."

She faced him in the middle of the room. "She knows just what I do. She was in bed when Mother left Tuesday night." There was an instant's hesitation, as though she was tempted to add something to this. Sader was aware of prickling impatience, sensing a fact being withheld. Then Kay sat down, indicating a chair for him. "Annie's been with us for years. She's an extremely motherly woman. She never had a family of her own. She emigrated from England when she was a girl. She talks often of going back there, and she has spells of sticking to her position, as she calls it. At such times she's a bit formal in manner. Sometimes she and Mother had little spats. Annie can be dictatorial in a sweet way."

Sader could well imagine the dignified, motherly Annie running the house to suit herself. "Did you ask her if she'd heard a car in Scotland Place at about the time your mother left?"

Kay shook her head. "She would have mentioned it. You mean, the taxi?"

"I don't believe your mother took a taxi. And belatedly, I found she didn't ride the Ocean Avenue bus downtown, either. Could someone have picked her up?"

"You mean, a friend happening by? It doesn't seem likely."

"She didn't telephone a cab company," Sader pointed out. "She may have expected to hail one. That doesn't seem logical, though, considering how late it was. I keep wondering if, for some reason of her own, she deliberately misled you about the cab."

He saw fresh tears in the gray eyes and disliked himself heartily.

He added, "I've been wondering who advised you to go slow about making inquiries, who told you not to go to the police."

She bit her lip. "I wanted to do what Mother would prefer. She literally loathed the police. She had a run-in with them about a traffic fine; she said they were goons and liars. She said it right out in court."

Now Sader suddenly recalled where he had seen the photograph of Mrs. Wanderley. It had been printed in the local paper some months past, under a line that read something like *Society Matron in Tantrum before Bar*. He smiled a little to let Kay Wanderley know he didn't take it too seriously. "I think the time has come to bring the police in."

"But aren't you——" She broke off. Annie had stopped before the door.

"Dinner is served, Miss Kay."

They went into the dining room. The long mahogany table was set with a full formal service, snowy linen mats, sparkling crystal and china, ornate silver that looked old and well buffed from years of polishing. Candles glowed in tall silver holders. Sader felt awkward as he pulled out Kay's chair, pushed it under her as she sat down. He offered to do the same for Annie, but she smiled sweetly. "I'll serve, sir."

"Oh, just bring the food and sit down, Annie," said Kay.

Annie brought the soup and they began to eat it. Annie kept an eye on Kay as if the girl were a child who might be stubborn and have to be fed. When the soup was gone Annie took away the plates.

Kay said, "Aren't you going on with the job?"

"Yes," Sader answered, "I've just begun. But I want the police to know, to have a record of your mother's disappearance. Then if something comes in, something I'd have no chance of knowing, they'll fit it in." As he said this and waited for her answer, he was struck by a comparison between this case and the one involving young Ajoukian. Why did he have this sense of urgency over Mrs. Wanderley, and not about the junk-dealer's son? He rejected Dan's theory of snobbery and then found himself trying to explain his idea to Kay. "You see, with a woman, there's always an added risk beyond mugging and robbery. And frequently that added element leads to violence. If your mother turns up somewhere—"

Her gaze seemed turned inward, looking at such scenes as Sader could only guess.

"—in such condition that she isn't able to tell them what has happened to her, or even who she is; for example, too hysterical or ill—"

Kay's thoughts went a step beyond; he saw her lips form the word *dead* soundlessly.

"—then the police, looking through their records on missing people, will check with you. You'd want to know at once, wouldn't you, if your mother is found? It could be anywhere. She could have been taken to another town, even another state."

She sat rigid, unanswering, and he couldn't tell if he had made any impression. Annie came in with a roast of beef, which she carved expertly on a serving cart. She whittled the potato she allowed the girl, and Sader got the impression that Kay's every bite was carefully totted up in calories. No gravy, though he was given a double ladleful. Kay ate the lean meat, the vegetables, and salad without paying any attention to the food.

Annie said to Sader across the candle glow, "It's been ages since we had a guest to dinner." She smiled; but Sader decided that she wouldn't consider him as being in the same category as the Wanderleys' usual company. The remark had been made for the girl's benefit.

If Kay heard the remark, she ignored it. She finished the plate of food with an air of relief. Sader got the impression she was very near the breaking point. She had faced something, the possibility her mother might be dead, which she had denied to herself up until now. The dreadful word must be chasing itself in her head. Behind the exhaustion in her eyes he saw despair like a closing vise.

He pulled out her chair. "I've been a rude guest. I've spoiled dinner for you."

She stood, looked at him blankly. "Wait till tomorrow to tell the police. When I—when I turn it over to them, I'll know for sure. I'll give up hope."

"Do you want me to go on, then?"

"Of course." She led the way back toward the living room, but Sader stopped in the hall. He had a hunch that if he left now she might fall into bed where she belonged. Sweetly tyrannical Annie would see to that.

"I've got some more to do tonight," he said. "I'm going to run down your mother's bar-hopping friend, the one you said called her sometimes."

"Tina didn't see Mother Tuesday."

"I just want to talk to her," Sader said firmly. "What's the usual hangout this early in the evening?"

"Try the Starshine on Third between Pine and Locust."

He nodded. "I know the place." He'd been there for drinks when he had been a drinking man and remembered the place perfectly.

A few minutes later he stood outside her door, looking at the broad avenue, the big homes with their cheerful lights glowing through the rain. A long time ago he had had illusions of hoping to live here, a youthful dream of success crowned with the badge of fortune, a mansion facing the exclusive strip of bluff. Now it didn't seem to matter much. He drew on his cigarette thoughtfully. These homes, big and imposing as they were, looked old-fashioned compared to newer districts being built by the wealthy. As Dan had said, a few miles away in Garden Grove you could have a mock ranch on one and a half acres. And your neighbors weren't elderly and stuffy mortgage owners from Kansas; they were young doctors and dentists and super-merchants, and they'd be fun to meet over cocktails in somebody's imitation ghost-town saloon.

Sader laughed shortly and bitterly to himself, he couldn't have said why; except that the dwindling of his old ambitions seemed to deserve a farewell toast of humor.

His bare head was getting wet. He turned to touch the

door handle of his car and then changed his mind and went back into the short block that was Scotland Place. At the end of the street, past a white railing that stood out against the dark, he could see the empty blackness that must be the sea, and he suddenly smelled salt spray above the smell of the rain. He walked to the white railing, turned left into the walk that should lead to the terrace of the Wanderley house.

He found the flagstone paving, the furniture left out to bear the brunt of the storm. All the cushions were sodden; the awning above the swing flapped wetly. There was not much light out here, since the draperies were drawn over the windows in the house, but he made out that now the swing was empty. There was no roll that might be bedding. There was nothing resembling wet fur under a blanket, wet fur that might or might not be a beaver coat. A *good* beaver coat, he added to himself.

It's funny, he told himself, that even when I'm feeling sorriest for her I don't quite believe she's told me all she knows. She's holding something back. Maybe she's too scared to talk about it.

He went back to his car and drove downtown to the Starshine Bar where he inquired of the bartender if Tina Griffin was in the place. The bartender seemed to be a little deaf until Sader tipped him a dollar; then he decided that Mrs. Griffin wasn't here yet, but she would be. Maybe ten minutes. She'd gone home to feed her cat.

"I like people who are kind to animals," Sader said, and the bartender agreed that this was an admirable quality. Sader inquired whether the bartender might tip him off when Mrs. Griffin came in, and the bartender looked deaf again and had to be revived with another tip.

With the dollar in his hand, he asked, "What's it about?"

"Nothing to do with Mrs. Griffin, actually. I'm trying to find a lost friend of hers."

"Mrs. Wanderley?"

Sader's face grew still. "What do you know about it?"

"Just what Mrs. Griffin was telling me this afternoon. Missing friend. I know her. Mrs. Wanderley's been in here a lot of times."

"Drink much?"

The bartender looked thoughtfully at the dollar, but Sader made no further move toward his wallet. The bartender said, "Sometimes. She couldn't handle it, when she did. She's got an ugly temper." This was a dollar's worth, so the bartender asked Sader what he wanted, brought the drink, and went away again. Sader waited.

Some instinct told him who she was, even before the bartender caught her eye significantly and jerked a head in Sader's direction. He could not place the source of his instinctive recognition. There was no aura about her suggesting the female bar fly. She was a slim woman with black hair, frosted now with rain. She wore a red plastic raincoat over some other dark wrap. She had neat ankles, small slender feet. She brought with her a kind of electric presence, and Sader thought that perhaps in summing up Mrs. Wanderley from her photograph, he'd decided subconsciously that this was the type of woman she'd try to run around with. There was contrast between them. Mrs. Griffin put up no show of pouting bee-stung mouth, no fuzzy mist of hair. She had fine white skin and brown eyes set widely apart and somewhat tilted, and with these items she somehow created an impression of exotic good looks.

She came directly to Sader's stool at the bar. She seemed to be smiling to herself. "You've irritated Charlie Ott almost into a fit. What are you going to do to me?"

Sader thought, well, that gets rid of a lot of preliminaries. He said, "May I buy you a drink?"

She sat down on the stool next to his. "What's that you're having?"

"Ginger ale."

The brown eyes looked at him quickly from under thick dark lashes. "With nothing in it?"

"That's right."

She thought about it while Sader offered her a cigarette and lit it. "I'll have a waterball," she decided. The bartender came over and she told him what she wanted. He looked as if he'd heard it before. She turned to Sader. "Now. Down to business. What do you want to know?"

"Do you have any idea where Mrs. Wanderley might be?"

"Oh, quite a few." She tapped the cigarette into a tray, loosened the throat of the red raincoat, pushed back a strand of hair. "But Kay knows all those places I'd think of. She must have checked them."

"Name one," he invited.

He thought he saw laughter in the depths of her eyes. "There's the pig concession." She expected him to ask her to repeat this insanity but he was stubborn.

He nodded evenly. "Could we go there tonight?"

CHAPTER FOUR

As they left the shelter of the Starshine's entry, the rain swept down on them. It was changing now to a fine blowing mist. Mrs. Griffin looked at Sader with the sidewise glance. "You aren't wearing any hat."

"Neither are you. On you, it's becoming." He touched her arm at the curb. "How did you know who I was when you came in?"

"Oh, Charlie Ott described you to a *T*. And with venom, I might add. Of course he's an awful old hen of a man." Again she gave the impression of sly, silent laughter. "Aren't you curious as to where we're going?"

"Just lead me there."

She took him to Pine Avenue, turned south toward the beach. This was the center of Long Beach's downtown business district. The store windows were brilliantly lit, but nobody was looking in at them. For two blocks Sader walked with her; they crossed First Street and came to the intersection of Pine and Ocean. It was busy here, because of the concentration of theaters and restaurants along

Ocean Avenue. Pedestrians hurried past under umbrellas. Wet tires sang in the street. From a corner drugstore floated the smell of fresh coffee. Mrs. Griffin paused at the light. "Can't you guess, now?"

Ahead of them, Pine Avenue ended in a short block that slanted steeply down to the beach. He saw through the rain the curve of lights on the circling pier, the indistinct glow which was the amusement zone. "The Pike?" She had said *the pig concession,* and he tried to imagine an amusement in which one participated with—or for—pigs. Perhaps the price of pork had changed the nature of the prizes offered in the games of darts and bingo. She hadn't said ham or bacon, though. The word most distinctly had been *pig.*

He met Mrs. Griffin's exotically slanted eyes and pleased her by showing his helpless mystification. At the same time, he was sizing up the woman. She was younger than Mrs. Wanderley. He would not have placed her age above thirty-five. Of course, Kay had said that her mother didn't look her age, so the two may not have been an ill-assorted pair, one black-haired and slightly oriental in appearance, the other fluffy, blonde, and pouting.

She was quick to see his study of her. "Is my lipstick on crooked, or something?"

"No. I was wondering about that Chinese father of yours."

She laughed aloud now in genuine pleasure. He saw that she loved puzzling people, that she possessed a sly sense of mischief. "That's my deep, dark secret," she told him. "Come along now."

They went down the sloping sidewalk to the level of the beach, turned right through a short arcade into the garish lights of the amusement zone. The noise was muted tonight, there was a pall of quiet, and the smells from the open-fronted cafés hadn't their usual fierce burnt-onion tang. The customers were mostly rather lost-looking sailors, obviously killing time. Sader looked in at the penny arcade in passing; there was a great jangle of music, but the idle cashier in her cage met his gaze stonily.

"The rain has kept everyone away," Mrs. Griffin said. She hesitated for a moment. "He won't be down here."

"Let's see this pig place, anyway," Sader said. "I'm curious."

At the end of the block they turned left. Ahead was the spindling framework of the roller coaster, its high lights lost up in the blowing rain. Mrs. Griffin stopped before a small booth in a row of concessions. A single light bulb burned in the wall; but as she had speculated, the owner and his array of goods to be won were missing.

Sader examined the set-up inside the concession with interest. He recalled something much like it down here when he had come as a kid. The booth was perhaps thirty feet in depth. At its rear, at about eye level, were five little barred pens, supported on some sort of framework that was covered in bright red bunting. Above each little pen was a mounted target, red and white circles surrounding a bull's-eye painted gilt. In front of the pens was a narrow ramp, leading from left and right at a slight angle to end at the middle at the top of a child's slide.

A sign painted on white oilcloth, hung from the ceiling across the room, said:

!! GIVE THE PIGS A SLIDE !!
3 BALLS 25¢

"I get it," said Sader. "You hit the center of the target with a baseball and a pig comes out and runs to the slide and slides down it. The owner gives the pig a bite to eat, so he won't mind coming down again next time. The sucker wins a plaster ashtray worth one tenth of a cent, plus a feeling of happiness over having given the pig a thrill. They've had something like this, off and on, down here for years. What puzzles me is that the suckers still go for it." He took a long look at Mrs. Griffin. "This is a place Mrs. Wanderley might be?"

Her eyes hardened, meeting his. "I thought you ought to talk to the man, that's all."

"Who is he?"

She turned her head slightly. "You ought to meet him," she evaded.

"Look, this business of your friend being missing is a pretty serious affair."

"I'm taking it seriously," she insisted.

"You're playing games."

A lash of color showed in her cheeks, as if he'd struck her. "I thought a detective would want to draw his own conclusions. I can take you to this man. I'd be a fool to tell you how to size him up."

"All right." Sader controlled his anger. "I'll meet him. Where is he when he isn't selling baseballs at three for a quarter?"

"He lives on Signal Hill."

Sader felt his face twitch. Mrs. Griffin did not seem to notice. They turned their backs on the empty booth, the lonely little cages, and walked up the broad cement stairs at Pacific Avenue, and so back to Ocean. Inside ten minutes, Sader and Mrs. Griffin were at his car.

She held back a little. "I could drive my own, follow you."

"This will be quicker." He held the door for her; she entered quickly. When he got in behind the wheel, he saw that she was rubbing her wet hair with a handkerchief. Her face looked set, disappointed, as if Sader hadn't come up to her expectations. It occurred to Sader that she might be a little drunk, just enough to put an unreasonable edge to her temper.

He drove over to Cherry Avenue. The town was quieting under the rainy night; traffic was sparse. He took the Cherry Avenue grade to the top of the Hill, and when they were almost at the summit, he said, "You'll have to tell me where to go."

"Turn right at the next corner."

After some blocks on the paved street, which led to the very crest, she had him turn off into a dirt track. Sader looked about, trying to fix the route in his memory. He could make out the black skeletons of oil rigs in the mist, and here and there a tank shone out with a silvery bulk against the dark. Below and to the right, the carpet of lights that was Long Beach made a fuzzy glow all the way to the edge of the Pacific.

"Park here," she said suddenly.

Sader had just caught sight of the house in the glow of his headlights. In the glimpse he got before she had him draw off the street to park, he thought the place looked old-fashioned, small, and shabby. It would be, he thought, up here. Nobody had built on Signal Hill, the part where the rigs were, since oil was found here back in the early twenties.

Mrs. Griffin touched his hand on the wheel. Her fingers were unexpectedly soft, warm, clinging. Mrs. Griffin had not done any hard work for a long time, if ever, Sader thought in that instant. The next moment, in the dash light, he saw that she was leaning forward and that the sly amusement dwelt again in her eyes. "You don't like people to keep you in suspense," she said. "I should have just told you flatly what I knew and let you come up here alone. Only, you see, I've never met a real detective before. And I am worried about Felicia."

Perhaps she was, in her own way, trying to make amends, to get them back again on the first friendly basis. He said, "Detectives aren't half as glamorous in real life as they are on TV, or in the movies."

"I think you're very nice."

"Thanks." He felt suddenly awkward and disliked her for somehow making him feel a fool. He got out of the car, shut the door, went around and opened her side, and helped her out. The footing was muddy. All around in the dark was the soft chuckle of pumping engines. Water was running into a tank somewhere with a muted splash, and there was a strong smell of oil. Sader thought, here we are, right in the very middle of Long Beach, and as far as the surroundings go we might as well be on the other side of the world. An oil field is a place like no other place.

She had turned toward the panorama of lights, far below, a misty glow softened by the veil of the rain. "It's quite a town, isn't it?"

"I guess it is. I think sometimes I've been in it too long."

He sensed that her eyes slid around at him. "How long have you had an agency here?"

"Since the war. A little less than ten years." He took out cigarettes, offered her one, lit both with a match. "Before the war I had a wholesale magazine agency. Somehow I got the idea that being a private detective would be more exciting, and less work." He laughed without humor. "I was in Intelligence, in the Army. Cloak-and-dagger stuff. It gave me a totally distorted notion of what a detective's work was like."

"What is it like?" she asked.

"Mostly it's little frightened men who can't pay their bills, or big defiant men who won't support their families," Sader told her. "Once in a while it will be a blonde, and blackmail. Rarely it's something very dirty like pictures taken through a peephole."

"You can't meet many nice people," she commiserated.

He smiled at her in the dim, rainy light. "I find them now and then. Shall we see if your pig-owning friend is home?"

"All right. Maybe you'd better take my arm. I'm afraid I'll slip."

There was a sudden sense of companionship between them, Sader felt. He wondered if she felt as he did, shut in by the rain, the memories of a lifetime spread out there in the glow from the town. He held her arm, and they walked down the slight muddy slope to the front porch of the house. He smelled wet shrubbery, geraniums, he thought, amid the overall stench of oil. Mrs. Griffin stepped ahead, to rap at the door, whose pane showed a light.

A shadow drifted into place on the pane, a curtain was pulled back, a man looked out at them. He had a heavy face on which the flesh was sagging. Sparse blond hair. Big ears that caught the light behind him. He peered through the pane at Mrs. Griffin and then pulled the door open. "Hello, Tina."

"I've brought someone to see you." She stepped in, and he peered in turn at Sader in the doorway.

Sader offered his hand. "I'm a private detective, looking for Mrs. Wanderley. Sader's the name." The man took his hand uncertainly, let it go quickly. "Mrs. Griffin thought you might know something that would explain her disap-pearance."

He was heavily built, and he sagged all over as his face sagged. He looked as if he'd gotten fat, up to a point, and then started to melt. He wore blue slacks; they needed cleaning. His shirt was white cotton. It had been washed, put on with-out ironing. His bare feet were stuck into straw house slip-pers. He rubbed a hand over the thin yellow hair on his head and looked bewilderedly from Sader to Mrs. Griffin.

She said, "Mr. Sader, this is Milton Wanderley. He is Felicia's cousin."

Sader was jolted by surprise, and then he knew that this was the secret Mrs. Griffin had kept carefully because she loved not only to mystify but to end the mystery with a clash of cymbals. To find here the cousin of the woman who lived in that great house on Scotland Place—He was taking in the small shabby room, and something more, an incredible noise. Inside this house were pigs squealing.

"I'm pleased to meet you, Mr. Sader," said Milton Wanderley. "I guess I got confused for a minute. I hadn't heard that my cousin was gone."

"She disappeared Tuesday night," Sader said.

"Well. . . . Sit down, both of you." Milton hurried to arrange chairs. They were very old, mismatched, had once been bouncy with good springs and covered with mohair. Now they were slick with soil, and lumpy. The three of them sat down. Sader offered Milton Wanderley a cigarette.

"I don't smoke. I'll have a stick of gum, though." He took gum from his slacks pocket, unwrapped it slowly, folded it, and put it in his mouth. "Gee, I wish I could help you."

"Did you see your cousin Tuesday?"

The pale blue eyes flickered with the effort to think. "Let's see, on Mondays I don't open at all. There's never anything doing down there, you know, so soon after the weekend. Even Tuesdays . . ." He frowned, wrinkling brows so colorless that the hair seemed to be worn away. "Last Tuesday, I recall now, I didn't feel too good. I was wondering if I might open up, or not. I know that's the day, because it would of meant two days off in a row. Felicia came here just as I decided to get ready. I was putting the pigs in their box. It was close to seven o'clock."

Above Milton's voice, Sader caught other sounds. A lot of little feet running in a muffled trot. Grunts. Squeals. There was an odor, too, but it was faint. He noticed then that Milton had a deodorant candle burning on the round table in the middle of the room. A sign on the tin candleholder said *Smelz-off.* It must work pretty well, Sader thought. He said, "How was Mrs. Wanderley?"

"She was pretty drunk," said Milton, with a touch of embarrassment.

"How long did she stay?"

"Not very long. It was like a lot of other times—she gets liquored up and comes up here to cuss me out for being a disgrace to the family."

"Did she mention any other appointments?"

The pale eyes clouded again with the effort to remember. "I'm afraid not."

There was a sudden burst of trotting, a chorus of squeals. Sader couldn't hold the question back any longer. "Where do you keep them?"

"The pigs? Back there." Milton seemed surprised that Sader had guessed. "Would you like to take a look at them? They're cute little devils."

Sader expressed his interest, and Milton rose proudly. He led the way through a hall, past the open door of the room in which he must sleep. There was a narrow bed made up with a patchwork quilt, a lighted bridge lamp, and, on the floor, a great bright fan of comic books. Next was the bath; it was dark, but Sader glimpsed the claw-footed white tub in the gloom. Milton stopped before a shut door which should, according to the usual plan of places like this, lead to the rear bedroom. He said, "Keep an eye out. They'll run through, trip you up, if they get away." He opened the door and clicked a light switch on the wall.

On the sawdust-covered floor, five little black-and-white pigs stood blinking at them.

Sader wanted to laugh. Behind him, he heard Tina Griffin suppress a giggle. There was something so cock-eyed, he thought, in the sight of those pigs shut in by rose-patterned wallpaper. Where the sawdust had thinned in spots, he saw battleship linoleum. It all looked very clean, as clean as it could with five little pigs living here. There was a white-painted trough, a regular pig trough, and a pan of clean water in one corner.

"Why do you keep them inside?" Sader wondered.

"Got to," Milton explained. "Two reasons. One, nobody's supposed to keep pigs inside the city limits. Of course this isn't Long Beach, it's Signal Hill—separate, you know. But the health officer's just as stuffy. So I have to hide them. That isn't all. I lost several pigs in the oil sumps around here. It's awful hard to keep a little pig from going under a fence."

The pigs made a sudden concerted dash for the door. Milton slammed it shut. "They're quicker'n lightning," he complained. "But they are cute, aren't they?"

"Yes, they are." Sader meant it. There was something impish and appealing about the little animals. "Don't they get too big for your concession in time, though?"

"Right along." Milton led the way back to the front room.

"I have to keep selling, and buying new ones, littler ones. I hate it, too. I get fond of them. Some of them have a lot of personality. They get tame." He looked depressed all at once. He sat down with a sigh.

Sader sat down opposite. Tina Griffin wandered to the center table and leafed through a comic book idly, though Sader sensed that her attention was fixed on Milton and himself. Milton stared at Sader as if wondering what more Sader wanted of him. Sader began, "Mr. Wanderley, I hope I don't try your patience too much when I ask you to go back over your cousin's last visit here and try to remember every detail of it."

"That's okay. I just wish there was something unusual to remember."

"Why should she walk out, leave her home and her daughter like that?"

"You mean, just drop from sight?" Milton shook his head. "No, she sure didn't do that, Mr. Sader. She's too proud of the big house, of living there with the rich people. And she's fond of Kay, in spite of the way she jumps all over her when she gets mad. Felicia's a determined woman. Not as determined as that Annie, but plenty. If she's been gone since Tuesday, something's happened to her." He snapped his fingers suddenly. "I just got it, the thing that's been teasing me, a thing she said."

Sader's body grew tense inside the concealing coat. He felt a sudden stillness from Mrs. Griffin at the table.

"You know how a thing'll flutter around in your head," Milton apologized. "I kept trying to recall it. Well, Felicia read me the riot act for living off my pigs and living like one—she said—but there was something she added, she kept putting in, jabbing it at me. 'At least you aren't too dishonest. At least you don't come sneaking to rob somebody blind. They know they're just getting a silly pig on a slide and a penny prize. You aren't a skunk.'" Milton's sagging face turned a little pink. "She said a lot, all like that."

"That you're honest," Sader said slowly, trying to make something of it.

"That I don't cheat folks like some she knows," Milton added in triumph.

CHAPTER FIVE

Sader must have shown that he wasn't getting the signif-
icance out of this that Milton intended. Milton hurried
on, "If you knew the family background, you'd know how
unusual it was for Felicia to say anything good about me.
Felicia was trained to look on me and my family like we
was dirt. You haven't asked why it is my name is Wanderley, though I'm Felicia's cousin and Wanderley was her
married name. I guess it didn't occur to you to wonder."

"No, it didn't," Sader said, realizing the oddity.

"In the little Kansas town where we were both born,
there were just two families that counted, that owned
much of anything. And they were interrelated a lot. There
wasn't anybody else there to marry, for those people with
money." He smiled a little with dry humor. "One family was the Wanderleys. The Coopers were the other. My
mother and Felicia's were Coopers, two sisters. Felicia's
mother went off to Chicago for a visit and married an out-
sider there, a real rich man. My mother stayed home and

married a Wanderley. Out of all that money-crazy bunch, he was the one who was different."

Tina Griffin was looking over her shoulder at Milton. There was a moment of utter quiet, with no sound except the faint chuckle of engines in the distance, the drip outside from the eaves. Even the pigs were still. Sader wondered if they had gone to sleep.

Milton went on, "The town called my father a no-good dreamer. I was crazy about him. I guess Mother was, too. We were awfully poor. Dad wrote poetry and Mother took in washing. It was a disgrace, people said. If she'd been a prostitute, they couldn't have talked worse about her."

A fleeting smile, mixed with ironic pity, crossed Tina's face.

"I understand that Felicia Wanderley grew up here in Long Beach," Sader said.

"That's right. Her folks moved away from our little town when she was four or five. I didn't remember it, since I was only a baby. I'm younger'n Felicia by a few years. They had a house there, though, and they used to come back for a month or so in the summers. When I got old enough, they used to hire me for odd jobs. I guess Felicia's mother, being my aunt, took pity on us. But once Felicia's dad had me trimming a big tree in his backyard, and I put my weight on a rotten branch and fell. I landed pretty hard and hurt my neck. I've had headaches ever since." And Milton rubbed the scrawny patch of hair in a way that Sader realized was a protest against pain. "Doctors never could do anything. Not that my folks could afford much along that line. What I always hated—Felicia's dad knew about that tree. We found out later that the man who was supposed to trim it wouldn't tackle it. Eaten out from the core, he said."

Milton's tone was explanatory, seemingly without bitterness; but Sader wondered with a flash of interest just how deeply that old score rankled.

Milton said, "When Felicia grew up she married into the Wanderley family—but she didn't make the mistake my mother had. She got one with money, lots of money. But I knew she always hated it, that my name was the same then as hers. We were just trash in her eyes, Mother and Dad and me." Milton shrugged as if it hadn't mattered much to him. "When I came to Long Beach in 1949, she tried to make me stay with her and Kay, where she could keep an eye on me. But I had a little money, and I bought the pig concession."

Tina said softly, "You did the right thing, Milton. She had no business trying to run your life."

"It was the name," Milton explained, as if defending his missing cousin. "She was always worried that her friends might connect her with me because of the name."

"I can see now what you mean by saying that praise from Mrs. Wanderley would be unusual," Sader put in. "Obviously then on Tuesday night she was so angry over the activities of some other person that in comparison —and perhaps with a touch of guilty conscience—she felt your pig concession wasn't too terrible after all."

Milton's pale, confused gaze sharpened. "Yes, that's what I was trying to say."

"She gave no other clue as to what had made her mad?"

"No. Nothing. Just that I wasn't as rotten as some."

Sader sat quiet, in thought. He remembered the moment when he had first seen Mrs. Wanderley's photograph, the quick dislike, which he had been unable to quell. The picture had been full of a silly pretense; behind the unlined and yet somehow unyoung face, you sensed self-infatuation. You sensed also the years of dieting, of expensive beauty care. And yet, the result was ludicrous. That bee-stung mouth and fuzzy hair reminded him of nothing so much as movie stills of the vintage of 1920. He remembered vividly the pictures, cut from magazines, with which his older sister had plastered her bedroom walls. Somehow, Mrs. Wanderley had fallen in love with herself at the stage where she had resembled Mary Miles Minter, and had never grown up.

He pulled his thoughts back to more immediate questions. "How did she arrive? By taxi?"

Milton nodded. "I guess so. I heard a car pull away just before she knocked. After she'd stormed at me about the pigs, and about people who were even worse than I was, she asked me to run her home again. I said if I did, the pigs were going to be in the back seat. I wasn't going to take her all the way to Ocean Avenue and then have to come back here again before going to the Pike."

"What did she say to that?"

Milton's glance shifted uneasily. "She stomped out and slammed the door. When I left about fifteen minutes later, I didn't see any sign of her. She wasn't at the bus stop over on Cherry. Of course she could have hit it just right, got a bus as soon as she reached it. Didn't she turn up at home okay?"

"Apparently she got a ride, all right. At eleven o'clock she was at home and looked in on her daughter to tell her she was stepping out again." Sader tried to weigh Milton's worry. Was it honest confusion, anxiety? "So far as I can discover, she disappeared in the moment the door shut behind her."

"Did Kay tell you how drunk she was?"

"Miss Wanderley told me her mother didn't drink overly much." Sader did not miss the look of irony that passed between Milton and the woman by the table. "I asked, because in any disappearance, it's important to know if heavy drinking could be a factor. People who drink heavily black out, do things and have things done to them which sometimes bring a break with the past."

Their reactions interested Sader. Milton looked embarrassed, as if Felicia's intemperance posed the same sort of problem to him that his pigs had to her. Tina Griffin looked remote, almost bored. She was probably a woman who held her liquor well, Sader thought; but she would be indulgent toward a friend who didn't. The indulgence toward another wouldn't have any pity or sentiment mixed up in it, just the recognition of realities.

Milton said hesitantly, "Of course, something might have happened, something real bad. She might have got in a scrape. But she'd expect her money to get her out of it . . . the way she tried to fix that traffic summons."

"Four hours passed, or nearly, from the time she saw you until she spoke to Kay Wanderley about leaving. She could have sobered up on coffee and food by then."

"Yes, she could," Milton said mildly.

"It wouldn't have been like her," Tina put in. "I've been out with Felicia many a night, and I know. She was fine, if she didn't get off on some grievance. If something made her mad, it was like setting fire to a keg of kerosene. It had to burn itself out. Through many hours." Tina came over to Milton, sat down on the arm of his chair. "You know what I mean. You've borne the brunt of those crazy moods more than anybody."

"You have to try to understand her side of it, though," Milton said. "She was family-proud. And because she'd always had money, she couldn't understand a lot of the ways other people used to get it. She said my pigs were filthy and I was gypping people with penny prizes. She just couldn't get it through her head I had to do it to make a living."

Sader spent another half hour in conversation with Milton without turning up anything further of importance. The man seemed content, sunk into a rut of his own choosing. Felicia had been an annoyance down through the years, but he showed little resentment about this; and Sader judged that in his youth Milton had looked up to the pretty, spiteful girl and that the attitude of submission had never changed.

The one worry Milton seemed to have on his mind concerned his pigs. He got fond of them, and then they grew up and he had to get rid of them. He knew, of course, though he didn't say so, that the pets ended up in the butcher shops as bacon, hams, and chops.

Tina Griffin and Sader refused Milton's offer to make them some tea and serve cookies. Sader drove Mrs. Griffin back to the Starshine Bar. There he shared another drink with her–his was limeade this time, hers was another waterball–and they parted amicably. Walking away, he thought to himself that she had expected him to ask her for a date.

There was apparently no *Mr.* Griffin to be considered.

Sader went home to his apartment, put away the car, let himself in with his key and shed the coat, then relaxed with a cigarette before getting into bed. It was a neat, plain, but comfortably furnished place. Sader had chosen the stuff himself, and the colors ran to brown and green.

He thought about Mrs. Wanderley. He'd put in more than eight hours on the job already, and he felt himself possessed of only a few threads, nothing definite enough to be considered a lead. What he had heard from the bartender and from Tina Griffin concerning Mrs. Wanderley's drinking dismayed him.

When she was drinking she had a violent, unpredictable temper.

She'd been drinking Tuesday night.

He recalled Ott's speaking of her disgust and disappointment when the client had failed to show up for a view of Ott's house. Could this have triggered her into an alcoholic binge?

Again the coincidence flickered through his thoughts, Ott's knowing Ajoukian from years of drilling on the Hill. The stray item persisted, a nagging scrap, even as he prepared for bed.

The morning was gray and cloudy, threatening to rain again any minute. Sader made coffee in his kitchenette, scorched some toast, boiled eggs. He had no illusions about his cookery. It was lousy.

When he was through eating, he called Dan Scarborough. Dan lived at home with an elderly aunt. He didn't like to get up early, and when his aunt finally got him on the wire he sounded sleepy, so Sader judged she'd had to roust him out of bed.

"How was dinner?" Sader asked.

"You'll never find anything like it in that cafeteria," Dan said. "Not to mention the likes of Mrs. Ajoukian bending over your shoulder with a bottle of vino."

"Anything new on young Ajoukian?"

"I'm beginning to hope he never shows up."

"Snap out of it, Dan. He's been gone since Tuesday, it isn't looking good. When did they report him missing?"

"To the sheriff's office? Wednesday, A.M. Old Mr. Ajoukian took care of it. A sheriff's deputy rode out from Santa Ana, took down details. He said he'd let them know if something came in. Old Ajoukian waited until Friday with high hopes for the cops to find his son, then began to inquire around about how the missing-persons department worked and found out that practically all the recoveries are people who walk in and announce they aren't gone at all, they've just been over to Joe's bar, or someplace."

"Yeah. They don't have the personnel."

"Then it seems old Mr. Ajoukian got kind of panicked. He'd thought the whole Santa Ana sheriff's office was in a frenzy searching for his boy, and the truth hit him hard."

"Well, the taxpayers get what they pay for."

"So they explained to him, I gather. He wanted to hire

one of their cops, exclusively, and they told him there were such creatures as private detectives."

"How'd he pick us?"

"He didn't. He had some kind of fainting spell around that time and the son's wife took over. She thought it was silly in the first place, she says, to contact the sheriff in Santa Ana, Orange County, when her husband had last been seen headed in the direction of Long Beach."

"Logical—but it doesn't work that way," Sader said.

"No, I told her the report had to go in to local officers," Dan continued. "Anyway, she took the phone book and opened to the detective-agency listings in the yellow pages and played eeny-meeny-miney-mo and came up with us."

"I think you'll have to demand a photograph," Sader said, after a minute. "The one the old man let you look at, if there's no other. It seems logical now that Ajoukian didn't get to the Hill. Why don't you retrace his route into town and explore the bars on the way?"

"I know, Papa, I had it all laid out last night. I made them give me the picture."

"Meet me at the office around noon," Sader said.

"Sure. Did you find Mrs. Wanderley?"

"Hair nor hide," Sader grunted. "Good-bye."

"See you," said Dan cheerfully.

A half hour later Sader went out to his garage and got his car, drove downtown and turned left on Ocean Avenue. He went on out past the big apartment hotels and the park, to the district where the old-fashioned mansions stood along the bluff, and so to Scotland Place. He parked in the narrow cul-de-sac of the street, walked to the white railing, looked down. A flight of cement steps angled back and forth, and below was the beach. The gray water was rough. There was no one in sight but a man leading a dog.

He turned left and walked to Miss Wanderley's big front door.

She looked as if she had slept badly. The blonde hair was swept back and up, but the hand which had put in the pins had trembled. There was no makeup, no rhinestones. She had on a pink cotton housecoat, inside which her figure was softly molded in voluptuous lines. "Do you have any news?" She asked it before Sader was even inside the door.

He shook his head, and her face chilled. "I want to talk to you." He waited for her to precede him to the living room.

Instead she opened another door. "It's more cheerful in here." He saw what must be a sewing room. There was a chintz-cushioned wicker settee and two matching chairs. A big felt-covered table had patterns scattered on it, a portable sewing machine at one end. In a corner stood a dressmaker's dummy. Sader studied it and decided that it must match Kay Wanderley's measurements.

"Sit down," she said.

Sader took the settee, she perched on one of the chairs. He said, "There is one point you'd better understand quite clearly. When a disappearance turns out to involve a felony, the police are pretty vexed about not having been told the person was gone."

Her throat worked. "What does that mean?"

"If your mother is dead, they're going to ask you why you didn't report her absence."

"You—you think something terrible has happened to her, don't you?"

"The people I talked to yesterday and last night don't seem to believe your mother would have walked out on her old life, on you, or on her wealth."

Kay's gray eyes held a heavy, wretched expression. "No, I don't think she would have, either. Unless——"

"Unless, perhaps, in a drunken rage she'd done something she knew would get her into trouble she couldn't buy her way out of?"

Kay put her elbow on the arm of the wicker chair, laid her forehead on her palm. "She expected too much of money," she said in a whisper.

Sader asked conversationally, "How drunk was she at eleven o'clock?"

"Pretty bad."

"Staggering?"

"Unsteady."

"Just what were her exact words to you?"

Kay looked at him miserably. "She wasn't always like this. Vulgar. Before she began to drink heavily——"

Sader cut in. "Wait a minute. You don't have to beat around the bush. I'm not passing judgment on your mother. I'm hired to find her. That's all. Now—what were her exact words when she looked in at you in that bathroom?"

"I heard the latch click and looked back from where I stood washing hose in the basin. Mother was leaning in the doorway. She was dressed as I told you she was. In addition, she had a gun in her hand."

Sader stared at the girl as if she were crazy. What a thing to hold back until now!

"She waved the gun around. She said, 'I'm going up there and scare the son of a bitch out of his wits. That'll teach him.'"

"And you let her go?"

"The gun was one my father had had for years. Long ago I disposed of all the ammunition for it."

The dutiful and frightened child, Sader thought, looking after Mama who just might take a notion to shoot up the town if she'd had enough to drink.

"What else?" Sader asked.

"I begged her to stay at home, to go to bed. Then I ran to get Annie to help me keep her here. That's when she disappeared."

Sader thought about it. "You're sure she didn't have any bullets for the gun?"

"I'm sure."

Of course, Sader thought, the man Mrs. Wanderley had gone to frighten wouldn't know the gun was empty. He groaned to himself as the possibilities opened before him. Then suddenly he forced himself to snap out of it. He said to Kay Wanderley, "Go to the phone and call the police."

CHAPTER SIX

She began to cry, rocking forward on the chair arm, the tendrils of blonde hair escaping to fall on her neck. Sader watched her for a few minutes, waiting for her to regain control; in his mind he said some uncomplimentary things about Felicia Wanderley.

Finally Kay wiped her eyes and lifted her head. "Will you phone them? I can't. I . . . . I couldn't talk coherently."

"It should be a member of the family. What about Annie?"

Kay controlled a spasm of sobbing. "Ask her. She's upstairs."

He found Annie in a big bedroom upstairs. Through the open door he saw her at a dressing table, before a mirror as big as a moon. On the glass-topped surface where she was working stood a vast array of perfumes and lotions; below was a pleated skirt of gold taffeta. He went in. The bed stood at the right; it had a gold lace spread. Underfoot was the silkiness of the white velvet rug. "Is this Mrs. Wanderley's room?"

She turned, the dustcloth in her hand. "That's right, sir."

"Do you mind if I glance through the closet?"

The question seemed to shock her. "Oh, I'm sure you shouldn't!"

Sader yearned to see if there was a beaver coat among the other garments, but couldn't tell this to Annie. Under Annie's soft politeness was a whim of steel and a rigid sense of propriety. Sader explained why she should call the police and report the disappearance of Mrs. Wanderley. But when he had finished, Annie was shaking her head at him.

"After all that child has gone through, there'll be no police harassing her. And no scandal. Not if I can help it."

"You're inviting a worse scandal. Hell will pop if something's happened to Mrs. Wanderley, and her daughter appears to have covered up her absence."

"They can't blame Miss Kay!"

"They will blame her," Sader said grimly. "They'll be most suspicious of her. It will be something the papers can hop on, too. None of the stuff they print will be flattering to Kay or her mother."

Annie dropped the duster among the bottles. "Do you mean that you can't handle the job?"

"It's not that. I'm not quitting. But I want my client, Kay Wanderley, protected. Don't get the idea the police will swarm out here with sirens blowing. The missing-persons department does as good a job as it can, but the police don't have the personnel to do much about a case like Mrs. Wanderley's. They'll take down the facts, put them on the teletype, make a few phone calls, and perhaps a detective might spend a half day talking to her friends."

Annie seemed reluctant to become reassured. "Miss Kay mustn't be hounded. It's not my place to gossip about my employer, but you should know a few things. Miss Kay has given up all her lovely friends, shut herself away, trying to keep other people from finding out about her unfortunate mother."

Sader nodded. Kay's life must have been bleak these last few years, he thought. And the chore she'd set herself was a hopeless one. Gossip wasn't to be downed nor outwitted. "Make the call," he said to Annie.

"Against my better judgment. But I'll do it."

He found Kay waiting for him in the hall. "I forgot to tell you—Mr. Ott phoned late last night. He expressed his sympathy. Then he said he'd appreciate it if I kept my private detective off his back. Did you insult him?"

"Not that I remember." Sader offered the girl a cigarette; she shook her head. He lit one for himself. Some words spoken last night by Ott ran through his mind: *You know how real-estate people are . . . afraid you and the buyer might get together without them.* And add to that, he thought, Milton's quote of Mrs. Wanderley's remarks: *you don't come sneaking to rob somebody blind. You aren't a skunk.*

Mrs. Wanderley's buyer for Mr. Ott's duplex hadn't shown up. Had he interviewed Mr. Ott privately, had they made a deal to save the agent's commission?

Sader said, "Ott had a real-estate deal on with your mother. She was going to sell his place for him. Just how seriously did your mother take her business?"

Kay's gray eyes were a little puzzled. "She didn't need the money."

"That's not what I mean. How would she feel about being cheated out of a sale, the two principals getting together behind her back?"

"That's against the law," Kay said seriously. "I've heard Mother explain it. Once a client goes to an agent and the agent displays the properties, it's illegal—"

"Yes, I know that. But some people take the law rather lightly. How would she have reacted to such a situation?"

"She'd have been very angry," Kay said firmly.

Sader studied the girl, wondering how much she would let him dig out of her about her mother's drunken rages. Not much, he thought. The child was loyal to its parent. It was interesting to speculate, though, if Mrs. Wanderley had gone out Tuesday night waving a gun for Charlie Ott. "Well, I'll be going. I have a couple of things to check. Why don't you come down to my office around noon? My partner will be there. We're going to hash over the cases we're working on."

"You're working on more than one case?"

"No. He's doing a job of his own. We go over the stuff together. Sometimes you develop a blind spot about some part of your job, or get off on a wrong track. I want to talk to him about your mother, and I'd like to have you there. You might think of something to add."

She rubbed her hands together as if they were cold, then tucked her arms across her bosom. "I can't add anything."

"You might. Wear those earrings." Sader smiled at her and let himself out at the front door.

The dark sky was low overhead. There was a smell in the air as if rain was on its way again from the sea. Sader cast a glance at the heavy surf. Visibility was limited; not far from shore the sea and sky seemed to melt together in a watery union. He went to his car, got in. A heavy drop hit the windshield just as he put the key into the switch.

He let the motor idle, sat there deep in thought. Why didn't Kay Wanderley bring in the gaudy terrace furniture? It hadn't been meant for stormy days. What *had* the thing been, the roll that had looked like bedding, under which he had glimpsed a patch of fur?

I didn't ask her, he thought, because whenever she got close to that door yesterday, whenever she looked out there, something in her froze with fear. I'm too soft. I ought to go back and make her tell me what scared her like that. He reached a hand for the key.

Maybe I won't have to pin her down, he told himself, and left the key where it was.

He drove back to Cherry Avenue, up Cherry the long grade to the top of Signal Hill. Patches of low clouds lay here and there among the tops of the derricks. The smell of rain was almost stronger than the smell of oil. He turned slowly, searching for Milton Wanderley's house.

He saw it at last, down a slight slope. It looked very shabby in the dull gray light. He saw that on either side of the small porch, a tangle of geraniums, mixed with weeds, stretched to the corners of the house. In spite of the cold fall weather, there were a few straggly red blooms.

He saw no houses near Milton's. Two oil rigs backed up to what must be the rear property line, and some distance to the left were a couple of small tanks, painted with aluminum paint. It must have been there, Sader decided, that the water had been running last night.

He didn't turn off into the little road which led past Milton's house. He parked nearer the rim of the Hill and got out and looked down the long slope to the beginnings of houses and lawns. The bare earth was crisscrossed by winding tracks that led to rigs and tanks. The few patches of wild grass were brown, dead, and here and there they'd been burned off to reduce the fire hazard around the rigs. Far below, among other houses, he suddenly noticed Ott's duplex. Its fresh paint caused it to stand out brightly among the others. It was almost directly below, in a beeline from this spot. Of course no one could have made it by beeline, he thought, since there were precipitous banks, gullies, a maze of pipes.

There was also an oil sump, near an old rig above Ott's place. Not many of these were left, since drilling techniques had changed, the waste oil was carried away; and the old sumps were gradually being drained and filled. The surface of the oil gleamed under the pale light, black as obsidian.

He made out a fence shutting in the sump. In the old days you heard of animals and birds falling into these things. Even kids. He felt a stirring of uneasy tension, remembering those stories. Remembering the woman who was missing, the gray-eyed girl alone in the house in Scotland Place.

The stirring wouldn't die down, so he turned on it to refute it. The smell of the uncovered oil would have warned Mrs. Wanderley. Drunk or sober, you don't fall into an oil sump without difficulty. There were banks of earth, high ones, to retain the oil. You had to climb to get in.

Impossible. . . . He was turning away when his attention was caught by the tiny office facing a dirt road. He looked down at it carefully. It was a drilling field office, probably. He couldn't see any sign of life, but he got back into his car, returned to Cherry Avenue, drove down Cherry to a point opposite the military-academy grounds on the right. He turned left, through a fringe of neat houses with lawns around them, found himself on a semi-paved road that wound away among the rigs. He followed this until he came to the turnoff that led to the little office.

It was made of rough siding, with a corrugated steel roof. He parked in the open space before the door. A sign under the eaves said *Jenkins Drilling Company*. Sader went up the wooden steps and looked in through the pane in the upper half of the door.

The place was not deserted. A man in a green eyeshade was working on a set of books at a desk over by the windows. Sader rapped and walked in.

The man looked up at him casually, then took off his glasses and put them on the open ledger before him. "Yes, sir, what can I do for you?"

Sader took out his wallet and displayed his license. "I'm working on a missing-person case. I was wondering if by some chance anyone was here last Tuesday night."

The man rose slowly. He was slender, middle-sized, and looked as if he'd always worked indoors and without much exercise. "Tuesday? Let's see. What date was that?" He frowned at a calendar on the wall.

"It was the twenty-ninth," Sader told him.

"I always put in some extra time along toward the end of the month. I don't know about last Tuesday, though." The bookkeeper rubbed the side of his jaw. "Let me think."

Sader waited, leaning on the counter that divided the office and behind which were several desks and chairs, including the desk used by the bookkeeper.

"Gosh. Tuesday." The man went over to the calendar and studied it at close range as if it might tell him something. "I might have been here. I do usually put in extra time—I did last night."

Sader thought to himself that the man had an unusually poor memory. Tuesday was not so far away that nightwork should have been past recall. He said, "If you were here, would it have been as late as eleven?"

"Oh, not hardly as late as that."

"Well, thanks, anyway—"

The man interrupted by stepping quickly over to the counter. "What's it all about? Who is this missing person?"

"A woman."

The man frowned to himself again. "You think a woman was running around up here at eleven o'clock Tuesday night?" He went on looking puzzled for a minute or so, then all at once he grinned. "Oh, I get it. Necking, huh? Lovers' quarrel, maybe?"

"I don't think so," Sader said. "It doesn't stack up like that from what I've learned so far."

"Who was she?"

"I'm sorry, I can't tell you that."

The bookkeeper blinked. "But you wanted me to give you any information I might have had."

"The family is eager not to have any publicity," Sader explained, in as friendly a way as possible. "You can imagine how scandal starts and grows in anything like this. This woman was well-to-do, middle-aged, has a daughter." To himself, Sader thought that once the papers were out that afternoon, this fellow would know it all anyway. He pretended a sudden change of heart. "Oh, well, you might as well see her picture." He took out the snapshot Kay Wanderley had given him. It was a very clear print and showed Felicia Wanderley on the terrace in a pair of slacks and a sweater, her blonde hair tugged by the wind.

The bookkeeper whistled. "You call her middle-aged? Man, you need glasses."

"She's forty-seven, according to her daughter."

"Doesn't look it. You know, there's something sort of familiar about her. Looks like somebody I've seen . . . don't know where." He scratched the side of his neck. "Do you suppose she wore a fur coat over that outfit?"

Sader's face grew cold and alert. "Why do you ask?"

"Dunno." The man's nearsighted gaze remained blank. "Just occurred to me, you know; some women do. I think it looks crappy as hell, a fur coat over slacks that way, but they do it."

"You've seen her," Sader said firmly. "Where?"

"I tell you, I don't know!" The man's voice rose and his Adam's-apple bobbed up and down. "You quit trying to pin something on me!"

Sader controlled a sudden urge to mayhem. "There's nothing to get excited about. We think she dropped out of sight for some private reason and may be too embarrassed now to come home."

"I never saw her!" the bookkeeper cried loudly.

Sader kept his tone soothing, confidential. "There are so many possibilities, so many crosscurrents in a case like this. I've been running around talking to her friends. It turns out that she drinks a bit now and then. That could turn into something."

The bookkeeper licked his lips and regarded Sader with distrust. "I wasn't here Tuesday night, I just remembered."

"Too bad." Sader put away the picture; he noted that the man's eyes followed it all the way into his wallet. "I'm just doing a job. I'm sorry you misunderstood what I meant."

"Somebody'll get into trouble over her," the bookkeeper prophesied, "and it isn't going to be me. No, sir!"

"Why do you think there might be trouble?"

"How should I know? I read the papers. Some dame drops out of sight, catches up on her love life, or she's got to sneak an abortion—then she comes back home and needs an excuse for where she's been. So she makes up a yarn that she's been kidnapped, and then some poor devil who never saw her before goes to jail for fifteen years. Hell, it happens all the time!"

"Well, I don't think those cases fit Mrs. Wanderley's," Sader pointed out, watching to see if the name registered. "I think, personally, she may have done something a little reckless and she's waiting to see what will come of it."

"Like what?"

"A fight with one of her friends. Or taking up with a stranger for the evening. Something like that."

"Drunk driving, maybe," the bookkeeper offered gingerly.

"No, she wasn't out in her own car. I think she took a cab or a bus, but I can't trace them."

The bookkeeper was silent, thinking. Then he said, "I took for granted you were a cop. But you're not. What are you, a private dick?"

Sader showed him his identification again. "You were too far away to read it." He put one of his cards on the counter. "Keep this, will you? Call me if anything comes to mind."

"Sure, sure." The bookkeeper picked up the card, glanced at it carelessly, thrust it into his shirt pocket. "You had me worried. But I guess a private dick, he sort of plays it close to the vest. Besides that, you can't arrest anybody."

"No, I can't."

The nearsighted gaze was still innocent, still surprised. "Do you suppose there'd be a reward for information about this woman?"

Sader smiled a little. "How much do you want?"

"I haven't anything to sell, mister. I'm just asking."

To himself Sader said, *you know something.* He leaned on the counter. "We'll be fair."

"Who's *we*?"

"The daughter and myself."

The pale eyes wandered here and there, never quite meeting Sader's. "If I remember anything, I'll let you know."

"It isn't anything you can tell me now?"

"It isn't anything—period," said the bookkeeper. "I haven't remembered it yet." He went back to his desk, looked at Sader over his shoulder. "When I do, I'll telephone."

Sader didn't even say good-bye. He turned on his heel and walked out. It was silly to let a character like this one get you down, he told himself. But he had always hated people who clung to petty secrets, who tried to figure an angle for themselves before letting go of the truth. Something in their conversation had given the bookkeeper a whiff of money; Sader judged it may have been the fact that he was a private investigator, that the daughter cared enough about handling the case quietly to have hired him. He'd told the clerk merely that the missing woman was well-to-do; he hadn't said anything about Ocean Avenue or Scotland Place.

On the other hand, the bookkeeper's avarice may have been roused by the memory of a beaver coat. Mink, ermine, or sable would have been better, but as Kay Wanderley had said, her mother's coat was an unusually good one. A little heavy for Southern California. But a practical and sturdy sort of fur. . . .

And more suitable, perhaps, for wearing over slacks.

CHAPTER SEVEN

Walking to his car, Sader took out his notebook and turned the pages to his copy of Mrs. Wanderley's appointments. For Monday she'd written, *Margot's, drinks, 5.* He flipped on past a couple of sheets. Kay had jotted down neatly, *Mrs. Margot Cole, 3132 Redwood.* The address, as Kay had mentioned, was on the Hill; but not on this side of it. This south side, facing the city and the sea, dropped sharply. To the north was a more gradual slope, much more thickly worked. Concentrated there along Cherry Avenue were the tool companies, the drilling contractors, the field offices of big outfits like Texaco and Standard, even a couple of small refineries. It was the business district of the Hill, and Redwood wasn't over a block or two off Cherry.

With a sense of curiosity about the woman who lived in such a neighborhood, he turned the car northward.

He was surprised when he saw the place. Though the house figured to be at least thirty years old and was surrounded by working rigs and oil tanks, it wouldn't have been out of place on any quiet street in the residential sections. It was built of white stucco with a red tile roof; there was a neat lawn to the curb, a hedge of evergreens, a weeping willow. There was every indication of good care. A row of potted begonias and ferns lined the edge of the cement porch. Under the willow tree a white plaster mama duck led three little ducks in a parade.

A pickup truck went by, tools rattling in its bed. A steam whistle screeched from a refinery on Cherry. Not the quietest place on earth, Sader thought. But lots of privacy from the neighbors.

He parked the car at the edge of the street, went up the cement walk, and rang the bell. Almost at once he heard footsteps and then the door was pulled open by a woman.

He sized her up through the screen. She was about fifty and had coarse black hair pulled back into a knot. Her face was big-boned, its lines heavy, though her figure was pleasingly slim. The eyes were striking. They were the bluest Sader had ever seen, a color like bright paint, and the thick black lashes around them gave a look of shining through shadow. She wore a figured housecoat. "How do you do?"

Sader was pleased with her voice. You didn't often hear that soft, rich tone. "Sader's my name. I'm a private detective trying to trace your friend, Mrs. Wanderley."

"Yes, Mr. Sader, I've heard about that." She moved back and gestured for him to come in. "Excuse the house. I work nights, I don't get much housework done any more." She ran around picking up newspapers, then indicated a chair for him.

The front door opened right into the living room. Sader

could not see many signs of neglect, in spite of Mrs. Cole's apology. The furniture was not in the same class as Mrs. Wanderley's, but neither was it nondescript or shabby. There were more spindle-legged tables than he would have cared for, with white lace doilies and china figurines on them. Some African violets bloomed in a bright red pot over beside the window. The lace curtains looked crisply starched, immaculate. The brown rug hadn't a stray thread or a trace of lint. He said, "I hope I didn't interrupt your daytime nap."

She came back to sit down near him. "I'm getting so I'm just like a cat. I sleep in little snatches, all through the day. I know it isn't the right way to get a complete rest, but I can't help myself. I guess in the end I'll just have to get a day job."

"Some people can adjust to nightwork and some can't. If I were having trouble, I'd get out of it," Sader advised.

She nodded. "I feel that way, too. I've stayed on as long as I have because I like the work and the pay is good. I'm night receptionist at the hospital." She smoothed the skirt of the housecoat on her knee. "I guess you want to ask me about Felicia. Whether I know where she is. I don't." She lifted the strange blue eyes in a direct stare at Sader.

"Well, we might talk about her last visit here."

"That was Monday, nearly a week ago. It's awful how time flies." She shook her head slightly. "I invited a few friends here Monday afternoon. It's my night off. I served cocktails and a buffet snack."

"When did Mrs. Wanderley arrive?"

"A little after five. She was here a couple of hours, I suppose. They'd all gone by eight."

"You were lucky," Sader told her, smiling. "I've had friends come for five o'clock cocktails and have taken them home and poured them into bed about two A.M. the next morning."

She returned his smile. "Yes, I've had that happen too. But Felicia sort of put a frost on things. She was cross about something. Sometimes when she'd had enough to drink she went on rampages. I think everyone was a bit nervous, thinking of that."

"What had upset her?"

Mrs. Cole shook her head. "I don't know. She came in quiet enough. After she'd been here awhile, had talked to some of the others, she came out into the kitchen, following me when I went to replenish the drinks, and she wanted to talk to me about my . . . my divorce." For the first time Margot Cole's air of frankness broke down; she flashed him a look that was mostly defiance, and he judged that her resentment over Felicia's prying was still fresh. "I've known Felicia since we were kids in school. Thirty-five years, anyway. And we've been friends all that time. But I felt she was overstepping herself. She said that real-estate people know a lot of law, and that she could help me with advice about the divorce settlement, and I had to speak very plainly to her. I told her I'd left the arrangement of the property settlement to my attorney, in whom I have complete confidence."

From the heat in her voice Sader judged that his next question had better be phrased tactfully. "Perhaps her motive was kindly. Perhaps she thought you were being taken advantage of in some way."

Margot Cole laughed shortly. "How could she? I hadn't discussed my marriage or its breakup with her."

"I'd better explain something." Sader told her of the last scene between Kay and her mother, the gun and the threats to use it to scare somebody, and then of Mrs. Wanderley's enigmatic remarks to Milton. When he had concluded he added: "It seems she must have gone off in a towering rage over some sort of dishonesty. Even though you know of no information she might have had about your divorce settlement, it's possible she imagined some injustice was being done."

The blue eyes were direct and frosty. "I'll co-operate in every reasonable way, Mr. Sader, to help you find Felicia. But I won't have you dragging my private affairs into it, I won't have you poking into my divorce. I've gone out of my way to keep it quiet and respectable. My two children are enrolled in wonderful schools. I intend to see that no smear touches them. I might add that it's quite impossible that Felicia should be running around looking for my husband. He's in Texas."

Sader kept his tone smooth and friendly. "I'm in complete sympathy with you, Mrs. Cole. But perhaps she felt your attorney wasn't doing all that was possible."

"My attorney is a woman."

Sader saw no other avenue to pursue this lead. "Might I ask with whom Mrs. Wanderley talked here Monday evening?"

Some of her anger ebbed and she relaxed a little. "I noticed her once with Charlie Ott. Of course there is some kind of deal on between them, she's signed him up to sell his place, and I suppose they talked about that. He isn't the type she'd choose for banter. Tina Griffin and Felicia were together, I recall."

"Was Milton Wanderley among your guests?"

"No." She was looking at him curiously. "Did Kay have you look him up?"

"Mrs. Griffin took me to see him."

"I feel sorry for Milton. Felicia acts as if he's disgracing her with his pigs. He's just making a living in one of the few ways open to him."

Sader nodded. "You didn't notice Mrs. Wanderley with anyone except Mr. Ott and Mrs. Griffin?"

She started to answer and then checked herself. He saw that she was debating a question, and he remembered the man in the field office and made a bet with himself: this wasn't his day, and she'd clam up on him.

But she began to speak with an air of pulling the words out one by one from a sack, not sure what she'd draw next. "Felicia spoke to another man. His being here was an accident and concerned my divorce settlement. I saw Felicia and this man in the dining room where I had set up the buffet."

Sader had noticed the large alcove at the rear of the room, filled by a big oak table and leather-cushioned chairs.

"You hadn't wanted this man here because his business with you was private?" Sader hazarded.

"I haven't cared for my friends to know anything about my divorce or the settlement which was being arranged," Mrs. Cole said slowly. "I'm not just a perversely secretive woman, Mr. Sader. My husband was very unpopular with my old friends, for reasons I shan't go into here. That should explain to you why I have kept matters to myself and why I would have preferred Mr. Ajoukian not to have come that night."

Sader blinked. He felt as if some kind of eclipse, upheaval, or other startling phenomenon had taken place in an instant when he had turned his head. "What did you say?"

"I said that my husband was unpopular with my friends. Their attitude would be prejudiced."

"This man, this Ajoukian. Mrs. Wanderley spoke to him?"

"I think so."

"Do you think they might have known each other?"

"Previously, you mean? I have no idea."

"Was he introduced to her here?"

"I didn't introduce them. When Mr. Ajoukian came, most of the others had gone. He looked in and saw a half dozen or so in this room, and said he wouldn't interrupt a party; and then, not wishing to be rude, I asked if he would have a drink. He came in and I gave him a cocktail. Frankly, I didn't want to take him around to each of the others and give his name, and explain who he was. So I let him get along as best he could."

Sader could imagine Mrs. Cole's predicament. She hadn't wanted Ajoukian mixing with her friends but had been too squeamish to turn him off abruptly. No doubt she had feared he might drop some hint of the divorce settlement.

"Ajoukian's business was buying oil shares," Sader said. "Were you selling him some?"

"That has nothing to do with this matter of Felicia's disappearance."

"I'm not so sure. You see, young Mr. Ajoukian also dropped from sight last Tuesday."

He was surprised at the lack of response. The blue eyes remained fixed on his in placid determination to resist his probing. But she asked, "Are you investigating both of these disappearances?"

"Yes."

"That's odd."

"In what way?" Sader asked quickly.

"To be such a coincidence."

Sader looked at her thoughtfully. "You mean, for the families of the two who dropped from sight both to choose my agency?"

She nodded. "Of course there aren't a great many agencies of your sort in Long Beach. I'd guess a half dozen, perhaps."

"You've missed it by half."

She smiled slightly. "However, I suppose some of the dozen-odd don't look for missing persons. Some of them do private patrol, special police duties, that sort of thing."

"Yes, you're right. However, concerning this visit here by young Mr. Ajoukian—"

"No, you're mistaken. Young Mr. Ajoukian wasn't here at all."

Sader made one of his few vexatious gestures in impatience at his own hurry to jump at a conclusion: he pounded a fist once into the palm of his other hand. "The old man?"

"Yes." She turned her head a fraction of an inch, then caught herself. But Sader, noting the slight motion, was alerted to its cause. Somewhere in the rear of the house there had been a faint sound. A door had shut, almost silently. He judged from Mrs. Cole's attitude that she was fully aware of what was happening, that she didn't want him to know.

He gave no sign of wondering who might be back there. "Was Ajoukian's manner toward Mrs. Wanderley familiar? Friendly? Placating? Or what?"

"Mr. Sader, perhaps in your work you've learned to examine other people with an X-ray eye. Perhaps you discover all sorts of meanings in their casual social behavior. You see guilt, and anger, and terror, and evil intentions under their outward appearances. But I don't. When I glanced into the alcove and saw Felicia talking to Mr. Ajoukian, I thought only that they might have found a topic of common interest. Or at most, that she was being pleasant to an old and rather unattractive man."

Sader sighed. "I wish I did possess those X-ray eyes you mention. But why do you speak of evil intentions? On whose part?"

A brief flash of irritation crossed her features. "Certainly not on Mr. Ajoukian's."

"You felt no antagonism between them?"

She looked at him as if she considered him exceptionally stupid. "You keep hinting at a possibility of foul play. Forget it, Mr. Sader. Felicia was always perfectly capable of taking care of herself."

"Even when she'd been drinking heavily?"

"People got out of her way when she'd been drinking heavily," Mrs. Cole said in a sharp tone. "I wouldn't want such an idea to get back to Kay, but just between us, I think Felicia is having herself a spree. I know what Kay must have told you, that her mother was past the age for love affairs. Don't believe it."

Sader smiled. "Mrs. Wanderley had romantic notions?" This, then, was the first he'd heard of it.

"She was capable of falling for some man."

"You were such an old friend of hers—had you noticed any particular symptoms?"

She stiffened under his glance. "Don't ridicule what I'm saying."

"That was far from my intention."

He saw her eyes fixed on her wrist watch. "I wish I could help you find Felicia, but I can't. I have this theory, which I hope you won't repeat to Kay. That's all I can offer."

"I'll have to contact Mr. Ajoukian," Sader said, rising.

Real anger glittered in her strange blue eyes. "Do so without mentioning my name." She stood up to face him. He saw her clenched hands at her sides, the tension in her throat, her shoulders. She was like a cat suddenly set to pounce.

"I'll manage that," he agreed. "You had other guests here, I'll say that one of them mentioned Ajoukian's meeting Mrs. Wanderley."

He saw that this didn't satisfy her. She didn't want him seeing Ajoukian. There was an instant of angry silence, and in it Sader thought he heard a footfall. Whoever she had back there was being exceptionally quiet. Sader allowed no change to cross his face at the surreptitious sound.

"Please trust my discretion," he pleaded. "You don't have to be afraid I'll pry into your divorce."

She didn't relent. "My interest is in the welfare of my children."

The words followed him out into the gray light of the street, and he wondered at his own mistrust of them. There had been something flat and tinny in her tone, the ring of a false coin. He got into his car. Me and my X-ray ears, he jibed to himself. He looked back at Mrs. Cole's house. He wished he knew who it was who had waited and listened to their conversation, whose movements had been so stealthy, of whose presence Mrs. Cole had been so secretly aware. Somehow he thought the unseen one was a man.

No reason for this, he told himself—the act of eavesdropping, of prying and peeping, was more like a woman. Or it might have been one of Mrs. Cole's children, home from school.

He decided the impression that a man had been hiding out of sight in Mrs. Cole's back bedroom arose from her attitude toward her divorce. She wanted the settlement, the suit, to go smoothly and quietly. Not because of the kids, Sader speculated, but perhaps because of another love.

She was fifty, or nearly, and to someone like Kay Wanderley, in spite of her denials, fifty was doddering and sexless and past all thought of romance. Let Kay live, Sader thought; she'll learn it isn't so.

He took a last look at the willow, at the plaster ducks, the potted plants along Mrs. Cole's front porch. If I were having the kind of breaks the private dicks get on TV, he thought, young Ajoukian would sneak out of the house now and I'd nail him and he'd confess to murdering Mrs. Wanderley because she was going to tell his father on him and Mrs. Cole. Of course Mrs. Cole is old enough to be his mother; but he has a mother complex. He lost his so long ago, after she'd lived all those years in a shack behind the old man's tool yard.

Or maybe it went this way. . . .

He was still embroidering on it when he walked into his office and found Dan there with the taxi driver who had seen Mrs. Wanderley at five o'clock on Wednesday morning.

CHAPTER EIGHT

The taxi driver was a neat young man with thick dark hair and nervous eyes. He sat on the red leather lounge and twisted a uniform cap in his hands. "You understand, I'm trusting you to treat this confidentially."

Dan glanced at Sader. "Can you do it?"

"It depends on what he means," Sader said.

"It mustn't get in the paper," the taxi driver said firmly.

"I won't put it in," Sader said. "I can't promise for the cops, if it turns out something's happened to her."

"She was okay at five o'clock Wednesday morning. Well, I'll correct that—she said she had a cold. She was all wrapped up."

Sader took out the snapshot and handed it to him. "Is that the woman you saw on Wednesday morning?"

The driver examined the snapshot critically. "Well . . . she had on a fur coat, a scarf tied under her chin. I guess it's the same. The clothes matched the description you left in the dispatcher's office. She told me her name. Wanderley."

Dan's eyebrows shot up in surprise; he looked again at Sader. "How did that happen?"

"She just did," said the driver uneasily. "When she left the cab out at the Veterans' Hospital, she told me."

"Why do you want the trip kept quiet?" Sader asked.

"She—she accused me of something I didn't do. She said I got fresh with her. I think she'd been drinking. Anyway, drunk or sober, I don't want my wife to get hold of it. I'm having enough trouble at home."

"Start from the beginning," Sader said.

By the driver's increasing uneasiness, Sader judged that he was beginning to wish he hadn't come in. He shifted restlessly on the couch. "It seemed just a routine pickup. She signaled for me to stop on a corner below Pacific Coast Highway, near Cherry. She wanted a ride out to the Veterans' Hospital. I went out there by way of Anaheim Street. Nothing happened during the trip that I knew of. When we got to the hospital, I parked the cab in the taxi zone by the front gates and got out and opened the door for her. She took a bill out of her pocket; and I returned her change. She was coughing meanwhile in a handkerchief. When I gave her the change my hand accidentally touched hers and she said, 'You filthy beast, don't dare to touch me like that.' I said, 'Gee, I'm sorry, lady,' or something to apologize. But she coughed a little and then said, 'I saw you staring at me in the rear-view mirror. I know what you're up to.'" The driver suddenly waved the cap in desperation. "Honest to God, I didn't have any such idea!"

Sader said, "You think she'd been drinking?"

"What else? I hadn't been leering at her in the mirror. Touching her hand was an accident."

"How did she happen to tell you her name?"

The driver licked his lips nervously. "Standing there, early like that, me and her both nearly freezing, she said, 'Don't be surprised if your company hears from my lawyers. I'll see you busted or my name isn't'—well, I don't recall the first name, though she said it—'my name isn't Wanderley.'"

"Felicia Wanderley?" Sader suggested.

The driver nodded at once. "Yeah, that's it."

Dan asked, "What did she do then?"

"She kicked me," the driver blurted, and as if remembering the painful blow, leaned over to rub his shin. "Then she walked off, the coat swinging out wide behind her. I got a good look at that outfit you described in your bulletin, the white blouse and green slacks, a green scarf over her head."

Sader was rubbing the edge of the desk with his finger tip. "Handbag?"

The driver shook his head. "She didn't carry one."

"You said she took the bill out of her coat pocket?"

"That's right. It was a twenty."

"She put the change back into her pocket?"

"I guess so. Gosh, I was so surprised my head was swimming. I never had a dame haul off like that, not for something I hadn't even thought of doing."

Dan said, "Where did she go? Into the hospital grounds?"

"I didn't wait to see."

Sader took typing paper from a drawer of the desk. "If I write this up as you've told it to us, will you sign it?"

"If that's how I get the reward, okay."

Sader ran paper into the machine he raised from inside the desk. He typed, and Dan offered suggestions. The driver read what was written, signed it with Dan as witness, and received his reward. Sader warned him again that the police might make the matter public, but the money seemed to have restored the driver's optimism. "If it comes out, if the old lady starts raising hell, I've got this to rent a hotel room," he decided, grinning.

"Buses run out to the VA Hospital," Dan said.

The driver paused at the door. "Sure they do, and she might have taken one, but I don't know anything about it. 'Bye." He went out.

Sader put the driver's statement aside. "What about Ajoukian, Dan?"

"Wait a minute. What about this driver? Was he telling the truth?"

"I want to talk about Ajoukian, now, Dan. Mrs. Wanderley met the old man at a party on the afternoon of the day before she left home." He went on to fill in what Margot Cole had told him of the elder Ajoukian's arrival, his conversation with Mrs. Wanderley in the dining alcove. "Have you by any chance mentioned Mrs. Wanderley to the Ajoukians?"

Dan shook his head smugly. "You kept reminding me that there was no connection between the two disappearances."

"There may be none. But we'd better make sure. What did you find out this morning?"

"I had no trouble at all finding the bar young Ajoukian must have headed for as soon as he left home Tuesday night. It's out there in the country, a roadhouse sort of thing, only pretty high-class. It's called the Chuck-A-Luck Barbecue. There's a big dining room. Whatever they were cooking for lunch smelled good this morning. The bar is off to one side, nothing shabby or shady. The bartender knows young Ajoukian and between polishing glassware he confided Ajoukian, Jr., had a telephone call at about eleven o'clock. Now get this. Ajoukian left home at eight. He spent nearly three hours in the bar."

"Waiting?"

"The bartender thought so."

"Who called him? Man or woman?"

"The bartender strove and strove, but just couldn't remember. I tried to refresh him with a small remuneration, but he refused it. He'll accept when and if he remembers what we want him to."

"How does he place the time so well?"

"On account of a TV show. There's a set in the bar. He had to turn down the volume when young Ajoukian used the phone. There's no booth there."

"What happened then?"

"Young Ajoukian took off without a word. Merely settled his bill and waved a hand in farewell. There's one more scrap of information. Ajoukian, Jr., made the girls' eyes bug out. They drooled over him. I told you I figured he has what Valentino used to have."

"Yes, I recall it," Sader answered. "Where did the trail lead them?"

"Not to any other bar I could find," Dan complained. "I hit them all on the way in. I had the photo with me and I don't think they'd forget the guy. Wait a minute, you haven't seen it." Dan jerked open a desk drawer and took out an unframed portrait. It was about eight by eleven inches, matte finish, and as it slid toward him over the typewriter Sader glimpsed a man's face.

He straightened the picture and propped it against the typewriter keys. Young Ajoukian's dark eyes looked out at the world with amused nonchalance. The short nose, the firm lips were perfectly modeled, though he lacked any touch of prettiness. He was a thoroughly masculine creature, Sader thought, with somewhere a hint of coarseness, an animal vigor that verged on brutality. The black hair lay in a heavy wave. The throat was thick, well set. I wouldn't want to meet him in an alley, Sader told himself; and then added a correction: I hope Mrs. Wanderley didn't meet him in an alley.

"Bedroom eyes," Dan offered.

"He eats little girls alive," Sader agreed.

"They love it." Dan thumped the desk in sudden impatience. "You know, I've got the craziest feeling his old man doesn't like him."

"Jealous, probably. The old man worked for the money. The young one has the looks and the physique to enjoy it."

"I thought of one possible lead. Old man Ajoukian swears this is the only picture he has of his son. Usually photographers make up more than one. I'm going to try to find out where the other pictures went."

"Women, you mean?"

"Yeah."

"Before you start on it, work the Hill with that picture."

"Hell, I haven't run into anyone up there yet that doesn't know him, didn't know what he looked like."

Sader's expression was withdrawn and thoughtful. "I ought to go see Ajoukian, Sr. This Mrs. Cole isn't going to back up any play I make that might involve her. And Ajoukian may have his own motives for not wanting publicity on his deal with her. I'll be walking on eggs."

"Sure, go on out there," Dan said. "If it's going to be one case instead of two, we can switch jobs when we feel like it."

Sader glanced at him. "How come you're so willing?"

"It's Mrs. Ajoukian. I might as well admit it—I'm going to make a fool of myself around that girl."

There was a rapping on the outer door. Sader said, "This must be Miss Wanderley. I asked her here for a conference, hoping the three of us might kick it around and get some new angles."

"You're playing with fire, Papa. The clients like to think you're infallible."

"Well, I'm not." Sader got up and went through the outer room and opened the door. Kay Wanderley was in the hall. She wore a neat blue wool dress, a black Persian lamb jacket, a little hat of black velvet and sequins. The clothes were too old for her, Sader thought, too sophisticated. She hadn't worn the rhinestone jewelry, either; and in missing it he recognized what it had done for her. There had been something childish, youthfully optimistic, in all that sparkling glass.

"Come in, Miss Wanderley."

"I hope I'm not too early."

"You're right on time. My partner is in the other room."

He guided her into the second office; she looked around for an instant before stepping over and offering her hand to Dan as Sader introduced them. She sized Dan up with obvious interest. Dan was young, Sader reminded himself, with a frame unimpaired by experiments with opiates like alcohol. Sader felt suddenly older, more worn by life and more buried in cynicism. And as if across some abyss of time he saw the soft curve of Kay's cheek, as gentle as a child's. He told himself dryly that Dan's affliction in regard to feminine clients must be catching.

The office was warm; she slipped off her jacket. Sader handed her the portrait of young Ajoukian. "Did you ever see him?"

"I don't think so." She lifted her gaze. "Who is he?"

"His name is Ajoukian. His father made a lot of money in oil tools on Signal Hill, probably during the war when tools were hard to find. Now he and the son are in the business of buying oil shares. I think Ajoukian, Sr., was interested in buying something of the sort from Margot Cole. He met your mother at her house Monday evening at the end of a party."

The girl's eyes settled on the picture; she teased her lower lip with her teeth. Something about young Mr. Ajoukian seemed to fascinate her. Sader wondered if she felt the impact of the casual brutality he'd sensed.

"This man"—Sader bent to tap the picture—"disappeared on Tuesday night."

"You mean—left home, as Mother did?"

"That's right. He may have been on his way to Signal Hill from Garden Grove."

She seemed bewildered. "It doesn't seem to tie in."

"On the surface, no."

"Do you think there is a connection?"

"At first I'd have sworn there was none." Sader didn't miss Dan's sly lip-pursing. "But before we try to find a connection, we have another item. Your mother was seen at about five o'clock Wednesday morning by a cab driver who took her out to Veterans' Hospital."

Her bewilderment increased. "Why should she go way out there?"

"We don't know. We can speculate. The whole incident has a funny ring to it. It could be that your mother wanted to distract attention from her being on the Hill. She made a scene with the driver, frightened him and made him mad, and rather unnecessarily impressed him with her name."

Sudden color ran over the girl's fair skin. "She wasn't like that, when she wasn't drinking."

"Probably not. I don't think she was drunk, though."

Dan said, "Who did she know at Veterans' Hospital?"

"No one!"

"And visiting hours don't begin at five in the morning," Sader pointed out dryly. "But this was a time, and a destination, easily remembered."

The girl said, "If she didn't want anyone to connect her disappearance with the Hill—" Then she stopped; there was a minute or so of silence.

Dan said suddenly, "Look, suppose your mother ran into young Ajoukian up there Tuesday night and figured he was trying to gyp her friend, from something the old man said Monday, and engaged in a brawl that turned out . . .

uh . . . rather seriously. Maybe Ajoukian got hurt. She thinks he might sue her." He met Sader's cold stare and saw the girl's quick pallor and added hastily, "Don't get sore. I'm just talking off the top of my head, as they say."

"I'm sure that there is no connection between Mother and this young man," Kay said after a moment, and put the picture on the corner of Sader's desk. "She would not have the strength to injure anyone like him."

"Suppose, though," Dan persisted, "we find more evidence linking them. What do you want us to do? Ignore it?"

Her eyes on Dan were calm, not unfriendly. She had crushed down the panic and whatever emotion young Ajoukian's portrait had roused. Sader had an idea she was growing up all at once, fast. "I'll trust you to use good judgment," she said quietly.

Dan reached over, picked up the picture, squinted at it. "Was there any particular type of man your mother was attracted by? Like him, for instance?"

"He is good-looking," Kay said, "but my mother had no interest in romance in any of its–variations."

"No gentlemen friends?" Dan raised black brows in surprise.

He was getting the same reaction Sader had, yesterday. Frost. She shook her head, her eyes reproving. "No, none."

"She was rather an attractive woman, judging by her picture, to have given all that up."

Some stiffening, a defensive armor, seemed to leave her suddenly. "It was when she began to drink that I noticed she no longer craved the company of men. I'm not going to apologize to you for my mother's behavior. She wouldn't approve of it. She wouldn't even want me discussing it. But you might as well understand, since you're looking for her. She was raised in an atmosphere of immense family pride, and pride of wealth as well. While my father lived it must have seemed a complete, orderly, perfect world to her. Then he died, and she found herself an odd woman at social affairs, and all at once Long Beach was crowded with strangers, the city was crammed with newcomers who'd never heard of her. A couple of mild attachments she formed with men turned out badly. She took up selling real estate, mostly to pass time, and she saw a new side to life, trickery and knavery and sharp dealing. She grew impatient and quick-tempered. She—she started to drink."

This was a defense, Sader thought, which did credit to the child, an insight into the mother's deterioration that surprised him. But there was another picture painted by Kay's words, one she couldn't have intended, of a childish, spoiled woman too self-centered to adjust to loneliness and age.

"Now you understand," Kay said, her lips trembling.

"Sure," Dan agreed comfortingly. "And it must have been tough on you, seeing that happen to her."

"It isn't important," Kay replied. "Nothing is important now except finding her. Where is she?" She looked from Dan to Sader in worried appeal.

"I have no definite lead yet," Sader told her. "I would say, though, that the most important item to date seems to be the story told by the cab driver. That places your mother alive, and a free agent, much later than when you last saw her."

But Sader's innermost thoughts were disturbed by a strange hunch that the principal discovery was the reticence of the bookkeeper in the field office on the Hill. Under the coltish alarm he had sensed something else, the miasma of greed. The little man had the soul of a trader. And traders love to dicker. Sader reached for the picture of Ajoukian on Dan's desk.

"I'm going to borrow this." He opened a drawer of the desk, took out a manila envelope, put the picture in it. "By the way, Miss Wanderley—had you ever heard a story of how Milton Wanderley was injured?"

"Do you mean, when he fell from the tree? Yes, I've heard it."

Sader sat on the corner of his desk, the envelope twisting in his hands. "What did your mother think of it?"

"She said he'd fallen on his head and that it made him slow-witted."

"No hint of guilt? Milton says your grandfather knew the tree wasn't safe to work with."

She shook her head. "I hadn't heard it."

"Supposing it was true. Would it have preyed on her mind?"

Kay seemed surprised at the question. "I'm sure that it wouldn't. Why should she be blamed for something Grandfather did?"

"Her attitude toward Milton seemed pretty severe."

"She hated the idea of his using those pigs to make a

living," Kay said frankly. "I used to think she attached too much importance to it."

Sader nodded. He saw that Kay's loyalty to her mother would blind her to the woman's obvious coldness, self-interest, and vanity. He wondered for a moment if Milton's story of Felicia's last visit had been true. If Milton had had anything to do with her disappearance, the suggestion that she was angry over another's dishonesty would be a clever diversion.

Too clever, perhaps, for a man mentally dulled and tormented by the pain of an old head injury.

Summing up to himself, Sader felt that the conference had produced nothing to help them in finding Mrs. Wanderley. In fact, Kay's defiant insistence that there could be no connection between her mother and young Ajoukian seemed to cross out what he had done at Mrs. Cole's.

When Dan suggested that Kay should go to lunch with him, Sader agreed. She needed the company of somebody young, brash, and full of taunting good humor. He excused himself from joining them, saying he wanted to take Ajoukian's picture to somebody on the Hill.

The sky was gray, heavy; and there were a few pelting drops as he walked to his car. He drove up Cherry again, turned on the winding road that led past working rigs and scattered tanks to the little office where he had talked to the bookkeeper. The car crested a slight rise and he saw the building in the distance ahead of him.

A tan coupé was backing from the graveled space in front of the little office. Sader slowed down. The other car lurched back and hit a post, and he heard the metallic clang. The tan coupé dived forward, reversed again, missing the signpost but scraping a telephone pole.

"Crazy driver!" Sader muttered, his gaze sharpening. He noted the open office door, and something else, a cat's-cradle of torn vine, which had climbed beside the steps and now hung awry. With a twist of his wrist he turned his own wheel, set his car crosswise in the road. The tan coupé, free at last, sprang toward him. For an instant he expected a collision.

There was a nerve-jarring squeal of brakes. The tan coupé slewed to a stop. Sader opened the door beside him and stepped out, went around the rear of his car, and approached the other warily. He saw Tina Griffin behind the wheel, her face turned his way. You wouldn't have guessed the exotic tilt to her eyes, he thought, seeing them like this, narrowed in fear and rage. The black hair fell about her face like witch-locks.

"Let me past, damn you!" she screamed, her lips pulled back from her teeth.

"Hello, Mrs. Griffin," said Sader calmly.

His voice reached her and she seemed to pull out of shock, looking at him now in recognition. All expression left her face.

"Is something the matter?" Sader asked.

"Drive on and see for yourself."

CHAPTER NINE

The little office had in it besides the smell of almost rain and the miasma of oil, the dry bookish flavor of the opened ledgers. They were spread under the light, on the desk in the corner. The light shone on the clean white pages, the neat rows of figures, and on the man who had fallen from the chair and lay half under the desk with his legs folded beneath him. It was the bookkeeper, and he was dead. He was even a little cool to the touch. Sader put his fingertips on an outstretched hand, then drew them back. He went over to the office telephone on the counter, put a handkerchief on it to lift it, dialed the police.

Mrs. Griffin came back after a while. She climbed the steps and came in, averting her face from the corner where the dead man lay. "Was it . . . a bullet?"

"Looks like it," said Sader. He leaned on the counter and began lighting a cigarette.

"Give me one."

"Sorry. Forgot my manners." He gave her a cigarette and lit it for her.

She smoked for a minute. "Could it be suicide?"

"I don't see the gun, unless it's under him. I don't think he killed himself. I'm pretty sure he knew something about the disappearance of your friend."

Her face twitched; she rubbed her fingers across her lips. "Has he been dead quite a while?"

"Yes. By the way, when you were in here, did you notice any smell of gunfire?"

"No."

Sader waited, his eyes on hers; and some color came up into her pale cheeks. "The door was open when I came, the vines hanging as you saw them. I knocked. When nobody answered, I walked in. I–I lost control for a few minutes there." She tried to smile. "You'll say I'm crazy if I tell you why I came here."

"Maybe you came for the same reason I did," Sader offered. "I thought the man might have seen Felicia Wanderley Tuesday night. He admitted he worked late now and then. And this office is about midway between Charlie Ott's and Milton Wanderley's places, and they're two of the last people she had contact with."

She hesitated, then nodded. Sader wondered if she was glad of the logical story he had supplied, and whether he'd been a fool to supply it. "I've been running around asking questions. Not that I don't think you're doing a good job. Just . . . just playing a hunch."

"I haven't gotten anywhere yet."

She tapped her cigarette into a tray on the counter. "You called the police?"

"Yes."

"This—changes things, doesn't it?"

Sader's stare was flat, searching. "How?"

"Well, if he was murdered because he knew something about Felicia's disappearance—"

"I shouldn't have said anything about that. I have no use for an operator who jumps to hasty conclusions." Like Dan, gibed the inner voice. You didn't like it because Dan thought there might be a connection between Mrs. Wanderley and young Ajoukian, and said so. Maybe you're a little annoyed now, too, because of the way Kay looked at Dan in the office. Sader went restlessly to the door, looked out. The hanging vine was dried, full of dead leaves. He searched for something more, a shred of cloth, a torn wisp of hair, hoping that someone in flight had tangled here. But there was nothing. Behind him in the office Tina Griffin was speaking.

"Felicia was on the rocks. I wondered if you'd found that out yet."

He turned in the doorway to face her. She looked more like the woman in the Starshine Bar now. Some color had come into her face, and her glance was composed, and under the surface lay the hint of ironic humor—summoned now perhaps with effort—that had intrigued him last night. "You're so much younger than she, I can't help being puzzled by your being such close friends."

The slanted eyes met his for a moment, then drifted away. "I felt sorry for her. We are two of a kind. Maybe in her I saw myself, come fifteen years. I was raised in this town as she was. We both had such good solid Middle Western families, we both were kept so close before we were married. We never saw the Pike, we never ran around with sailors." She laughed briefly. "And then, most widows sleep alone—too long."

It was Sader who looked away, who felt embarrassment for her frankness.

She came closer, lifted her face. She wasn't wearing the raincoat, but a brief jacket of tawny wool, a red knitted dress under it. Her head was bare, the black hair blown and silky. "I liked you last night. Today you're like another man. You're afraid of me."

"I find corpses a little unnerving. Or maybe I too have been sleeping alone too many nights." He cupped her face between his hands, drew her lips up to his own, stopped with the first breath of contact. Come on, said the inner voice; who're you waiting for? Kay Wanderley?

The thin song of a siren lifted at the fringe of the Hill.

She pulled back, went to a corner furthest from the dead man's desk, sat down there on a chrome-and-leather chair. "It was a good try," she said. "Maybe I'll run into you again sometime, when you're not working."

Sader went over and gave her another cigarette. "Tell me, did you come here some other time?"

She nodded after a moment. "Last night. After you left me in the bar."

"How did that happen?"

"I was just driving around. I saw a light in this office."

"Was the bookkeeper here?"

"*That* man wasn't here." She flicked a glance toward the other side of the room. "The man who answered the door must have been the owner. He was awfully old and had on an expensive-looking suit. You know, you can tell good tailoring." She smoked in silence for a moment or so. "When I kept knocking, the shade was pulled back and a man looked out through the glass and said the place was closed. And would I please go away? I went."

"Why did you come back now?"

"Curiosity. There was something funny about the incident." She wrinkled her narrow dark brows in a frown. "He didn't give a damn what I wanted, what I had to say. How did he know there hadn't been an accident out here, people were dying, I needed the phone? Or that one of his oil wells was on fire and about to blow up? He had no questions at all. He just took for granted I was a nuisance to be chased off the premises."

"How late was this?" Sader was pacing now, back and forth by the counter.

"Oh, midnight by then, anyway."

"Did you notice a car parked in front?"

"I saw the end of one, I thought, sticking out from behind the place."

Sader excused himself and went outside, walked the graveled path to the rear of the office where he found a Ford sitting with its nose to the wall. He looked in at the steering post. The slip was turned so that he could read only the name, George Mullens. The doors of the car were locked.

Sader rubbed the graying hair over his temple, and thought about it. Mullens was obviously the bookkeeper, a quiet mousy type who might have entertained a secret itch like a yearning for fast ladies, or a love of horse racing. He'd had something to sell and he had wanted money so he had tried the market.

The highest bidder paid off with Death.

Sader thought wrathfully that there was no way to prove this, though it rolled through his mind with the clang of truth. There was another item on the first like a tail to a kite—his catching Mrs. Griffin running away. This was truth, too, as unprovable as the other: if he hadn't blocked that road she'd have been gone and the threat of hell itself wouldn't have wrung from her a confession that she had been here and found a dead man.

He roamed out into the weedy slope behind the parking space and saw some distance away the earth embankment and wire fence closing in the sump hole. He went over to it. The wire fence was in good shape, the embankment inside almost as high as his head. He was turning away when his glance skipped past the padlock and returned to it. He went to the gate and bent above the lock. It had looked all right at first glimpse because it had been hung carefully in place. Actually, it was broken.

He took it from the gate, went inside, scrambled up the incline. The smell of oil was heavy in the moist, still air. The black surface of the pool, as smooth as glass, reflected the sky, the shapes of rigs nearby, and his own peering head. There were a couple of bubbles out in the middle and that was all.

He left the enclosure, putting the lock back exactly as he had found it. Somebody was saving money, perhaps, or a pumper just hadn't had time to put in for a new lock. Sader went back to the drilling office and met the police at the door.

The man who interviewed Sader and Mrs. Griffin beside the steps of the office was about thirty, big, square-shouldered, dressed neatly and quietly in a dark blue suit. He had none of the characteristics usually associated with the police. His manner was mildly friendly, obliging, and he hid any tendency to display authority. He gave the impression of being eager to believe anything they wanted to tell him, so that he wouldn't have to delay them too long.

He reminded Sader of a hotel manager, or a cruise director, somebody whose power to order people around was submerged in a desire to keep them happy. He made Sader feel old and narrow-chested and dyspeptic.

This guy was good, Sader told himself, and their stories had better be accurate.

The officer smiled and put his hands in his pockets and told them his name was Pettis. He said this somewhat bashfully, but giving the idea that if they had any trouble at any time, it was a good name to remember and rely upon. "Lieutenant Pettis, to be accurate. But don't let that impress you. Will you tell me how you happened to come and find this Mullens together?"

Tina blurted, "I came first. I stumbled in on him and I . . . I panicked."

"Oh?" Pettis looked sympathetic. "Was this long before Mr. Sader came?"

"A minute or so. I was leaving when he arrived."

"You had a common purpose here?" His glance betrayed, ever so slightly, that they had better not be wanting wells drilled.

Sader told him briefly but clearly about Mrs. Wanderley's disappearance, and about her relative above and her real-estate client below. Pettis made arcs of his eyebrows, looked innocently up toward Milton's house and down toward Charlie Ott's. "Do you mean this man in there, this Mullens, had something to do with the disappearance you're working on?"

"No. I'm explaining why we both happened to come here. Mrs. Griffin is a close friend of Mrs. Wanderley's."

"You came here just because of the—the vicinity?"

"That's right," Sader said. "Mullens told me earlier today that he knew nothing, however."

"You didn't believe him?"

Sader shrugged. "I didn't believe, nor disbelieve. I had a photograph I wanted to show him." He let Pettis presume that the picture was that of Mrs. Wanderley. "He'll never identify it now, of course."

Pettis went back to the facts of Mrs. Griffin's arrival. Either he was wary of following Sader's lead into the Wanderley affair, or he figured the woman had more for him. Sader saw that Tina Griffin was frightened of the detective. She kept blinking her eyes and swallowing, and making nervous gestures with her hands. "Tell me," said Pettis, oozing kindness, "just what you did, and what you first noticed, when you got here."

"I saw the vine," she said, blurting it out as she had before. "It was all . . . all hung awry, as if somebody had hung on to it."

"You thought of someone hanging to it when you first saw it?"

"No. Of course not. I just—I don't know. I guess I thought the wind had blown it down."

Pettis looked thoughtfully and politely at the vine. "Wasn't it that way before?"

"No."

"Well, tell me about it."

She had to tell him then about coming late last night, and what had happened. Pettis spun a web of questions, but Sader thought she conducted herself well; he didn't notice any obvious inconsistencies. She was, he noted, apt to harp a bit on the well-dressed appearance of the old man who had peeped at her through the door, and Sader got the notion she was covering something else, afraid she'd mention it if she didn't concentrate on the good well-tailored suit and the expensive, highly shined shoes. When she mentioned these last, Pettis went up the steps and crossed into the office; and Sader groaned. She'd done herself proud up to now. Now she was ruined.

But no, not quite. She seemed to jerk herself together. "I must have gotten confused. Of course I couldn't see the man's feet. He was close to the door, pulling aside the blind." Pettis, inside, had just raised the blind on its roller from the halfway mark across the pane. When he heard Tina Griffin's correction, he came out again quickly.

"I wasn't trying to catch you," he said in a friendly manner.

Like hell you weren't, Sader said inwardly.

"Sometimes it helps to experiment, to visualize clearly." Pettis smiled at Tina, but she wasn't able to smile back. She was scared, Sader knew, and she was intelligent enough to catch on that it wouldn't do any good to try to hide her fear from this cop. "Now I'm going back inside, pull down the blind; and I want you to come and rap just as you did last night. And I want to stir your memory while we're acting out this little scene."

"The old man must have been the owner here," she stammered.

"Oh, I know the owner," Pettis said regretfully, "and he isn't him. See the name on the sign there? Jenkins. Old friend of our police department."

Tina Griffin had turned white. She had an obvious reluctance to do what Pettis wanted, too much fear of the cop not to obey. Sader smiled at her, trying to buck her up, but she seemed dazed and didn't appear to notice.

Pettis went inside. There was a minute's delay, a short time that seemed filled with a lot of muffled action within the office. Sader's scalp turned prickly and he felt the tendons jump in his arms and shoulders. He had an old hand's nose for trickery, and he was warned. For an instant he considered trying to warn the woman, even advising her not to do what Pettis had asked; but if they turned uncooperative they'd be under immediate suspicion. He forced himself to wait. Pettis's voice, somewhat indistinct, came through the closed door. "All right, Mrs. Griffin. Come up to the pane and rap."

She went wobbling up the steps, knocked; but the pane remained blank to her waiting, frightened stare. All at once there was a clatter that made her start with fright. The blind flew up, striking the frame at the top and turning in its sprocket several times with the force of the released spring.

Sader, below, grew cold with apprehension. Tina Griffin leaned toward the glass. She was rigid, teetering. He heard the slow hiss of her breath, the whimper as if with pain. Then she screamed and put her hands to her eyes and stumbled sidewise into the vine. She tangled there as if in a web, cried out, fought loose with a great scattering of dead leaves. With a face dead white, fixed, she fell down the steps into Sader's arms.

The door opened immediately. Pettis came down the steps at a run. Behind him, two ambulance attendants moved through the door with a covered stretcher. Pettis cried, "Gosh, I'm sorry! By accident she saw Mullens in there."

Sader grinned at him crookedly across Mrs. Griffin's shoulder. Tina was muffling screams against his coat. "Sure. Just by accident the shade flew up like a bat out of hell, and by accident the guy holding the corpse's feet had put down his end and the other one had lifted his, so Mullens was looking right out the door at a woman already scared out of her wits. I thought you were cleverer than that, Pettis."

Pettis's smile grew thin. "You're stretching the incident, Sader. I didn't intend to frighten her. I do notice, though, that she fell into the vine. If it had been on the wall, she'd have torn it loose as it was when she claims she got here."

Sader arched an eyebrow. "I see what you mean to prove. The vine was torn by someone who fell away from the door in fright—probably from seeing Mullens murdered. Mullens dead was out of sight behind the counter. But that puts Mrs. Griffin outside—"

"A witness," Pettis agreed smoothly.

Tina had caught the drift of the conversation. She wrenched herself from Sader's hold. "You're crazy. I found the man dead as I said I did. I didn't break the damned vine." All at once she was running toward her car at the edge of the paving. Sader tightened with expectation, but Pettis let her go.

The ambulance was pulling out then, too; and there was almost a collision.

Sader said, "Being a local cop, maybe you knew Mullens, too."

"Yes, I did."

"What kind of a guy was he?"

Pettis hesitated, sorting perhaps such information as he cared to give. "A bachelor. Lived with his mother not far from here. Crazy about gardening and cats."

"What about horses and women?"

Pettis stroked the line of his clean-shaven jaw. "I hadn't heard. Why do you ask?"

"He impressed me as having something to sell. For cash. I thought he might have had expensive tastes."

A flicker of recognition darted through Pettis's eyes. "His mother needs an operation."

"I guess that could be it." Sader lit a cigarette. "Do you want me any longer?"

"I guess not. Keep in touch." Pettis looked at the gray sky. "It's going to rain some more."

CHAPTER TEN

A burst of rain swept the street in front of Charlie Ott's duplex as Sader walked toward it. The wind was chilly. But the air that stole from Ott's house as he opened the door was too warm and too full of the smell of whiskey. Under the mop of fuzzy gray hair, Ott's face was pink.

"Sorry to bother you," Sader said.

"I don't care if you're sorry or not. Get off my porch," said Ott. "I got nothing for you."

"It's about the party at Mrs. Cole's house last Monday night."

Ott retreated behind the door. "I wasn't there long."

"You did see Ajoukian there, didn't you?"

An eye came into view, glaring anger. "No. If he came, it was after I'd gone home."

"Did you hold a conversation with Mrs. Wanderley?"

"Go to hell." The door slammed.

Sader went back to his car and headed through the rain toward Garden Grove. Once he was past the fringes of the city, the traffic lightened. There were places in the brown fields where the rain had gathered into pools. The orange groves looked fresh-washed, thriving. He turned on the car radio and let the thud of jazz underline his thoughts. Pettis wasn't through with Tina Griffin, of course. He had her on the run and if what she'd told him wasn't the truth, he'd break the truth out of her. Ott's behavior had seemed overly belligerent. It could be the drinking that had made him irascible. At their first meeting Sader had sensed in Ott an inner deterioration, a letting-down of barriers and standards. It happened sometimes without obvious cause. Ott, in possession of a well-kept piece of property worth a good chunk of change on today's market, shouldn't be plagued with the more mundane worries.

Into Sader's mind came a brief, unwilling memory of his own days as a problem drunk, with it a bitter taste, the sting of remembered humiliation. He forced his thoughts back to the matter at hand and began to check street names at intersections. The country had begun to look more settled, glossy, prosperous. A lot of well-to-do people were experimenting with a streamlined version of country life. The houses were big and ranchy, the out-buildings and fences gleamed with paint, the surviving orange trees looked self-consciously fruitful. The only chickens he noticed were some pure-bred Brahmas, big as turkeys, put out on a lawn to show them off. The rain had wet their black-and-white plumage a little, but not enough to spoil the show. The rooster by the fence gave Sader a hard look, and Sader said, "I'm just passing by," in apology.

He found the Ajoukian place at the end of a lane. The house was a white clapboard affair, roofed with redwood shakes, low and rambling. A grapefruit tree sat in the front yard, surrounded by dormant roses and shut off from the street by a split-rail fence. Sader drove into the graveled driveway and left his car, went up to the front door, and pushed the button and heard chimes ring far away.

She opened the door and Sader was aware of being unprepared. Dan had raved about her, of course; but somehow he hadn't visualized this creature. She was the most glittering silver blond Sader had ever seen. She had skin the color of cream, fine small features, a round chin with a big dimple. Her eyes were the soft brown of velvet. Inside the pale green sweater, the black skirt, she had a figure nobody ever whistled at—they might pucker up, Sader thought, but they'd be breathless. He said, "Mrs. Ajoukian?" She nodded, her glance curious. "My name is Sader."

The brown eyes searched him. "Mr. Scarborough's partner?"

"Yes."

"Come in, please."

She led him down a tiled hall. The walls were of glass brick and there were big brick planters full of greenery. It smelled of water and fertilizer. She paused before a door. "I'm taking you in to meet Mr. Ajoukian."

"Thanks, I'd like that."

She opened the door and Sader looked in on what seemed to be a square acre of gray carpeting, a fireplace built to barbecue a couple of steers, and scattered ranch-style furniture. Overhead was a beamed ceiling stained dark to look old and smoky. A bank of windows faced the grapefruit tree and the roses outside.

Over by the fireplace was a dark-skinned mummy wrapped in a white blanket. She led Sader that way.

The old man watched their approach with eyes like a bird's. He made coughing noises, then offered Sader his hand. His skin was cool, dry as dead leaves, and his nails scratched like the overgrown claws of an old hawk. "You found my son?" he asked hopefully.

Sader sat down facing them, loosened the raincoat, lit a cigarette. "No. I've come to ask questions."

"More questions?" The birdlike eyes pinned him with displeasure. "Connie and I have answered questions until we're hoarse. Can't you find my boy?"

"Not yet. I want to know about the party you attended at Margot Cole's."

"Mrs. Cole's?" Ajoukian licked his lips. "It's slipped my mind a bit. Last week, wasn't it?"

"Last Monday," Sader corrected. The old man was sparring.

"I dropped in after most of the guests had gone," Ajoukian said in a high, complaining tone. "Nothing happened of importance. Who told you I was there?"

"I just happened to hear of it. You met a Mrs. Wanderley there?"

In the seamed face shaded by the folded blanket there was any expression you cared to read. Smiles, frowns, grimaces, all were welded together in a network of lines.

Sader thought the old man's eyes grew cautious, but this could have been founded on previous expectation. The girl sat passively in the depths of a chair, watching old Mr. Ajoukian and Sader in turn.

"Yes, I guess I did."

"What did you talk about?"

The old man turned to the girl. "Connie, bring me a little brandy." As she rose, the silver hair catching the light, the old man's gaze dropped from her. "I've been laid up with a chill. Can't seem to get my strength." He looked at Sader to see what Sader meant to do.

"About Mrs. Wanderley."

The girl was gone. The old man leaned from the blanket. "She was drunk. She kept pestering me to find out what I wanted of Mrs. Cole."

"Did you tell her?"

"Of course not. The Cole woman's in trouble with her husband. She's selling what she's got on the quiet. She doesn't want anybody to know."

"No figures were mentioned, no amount of money?"

Ajoukian shook his head firmly. Inside the collar of his robe, his throat worked as if he were swallowing something. Nervousness, perhaps. "I wouldn't tell Mrs. Wanderley anything. Why should I? And what's she got to do with my son Perry?"

"I don't know. Nothing, maybe. She disappeared Tuesday night, at least she left home Tuesday night and didn't come back. She was on the Hill sometime during Tuesday evening."

"So were a lot of people." The old man's fingers strayed

over the fringe of the blanket, twisting it through his knuckles. "What connection have you proved?"

"None so far," Sader said patiently. "Except through you, your meeting Mrs. Wanderley at the party the night before her disappearance."

The black eyes under parchment lids took on a fixity of stone. "Is somebody paying you to find this Mrs. Wanderley?"

"Yes."

"You're looking for her instead of Perry?"

"My partner, Scarborough, is doing everything he can to find your son, Mr. Ajoukian. He traced Perry to a bar on the way to Long Beach. Your son stayed there until almost eleven o'clock on Tuesday night. Then he received a telephone call and left."

The old man took a handkerchief from his robe and coughed into it.

"I can't help wondering if the call might not first have been put through to his home here, that information was given where to reach him."

Sader waited; the old man fumbled with his handkerchief.

"Did you receive a call for your son, Mr. Ajoukian?"

"No, sir."

Mrs. Ajoukian came in at that moment, a small tray in her hands. "I took the liberty—" She smiled, gave Sader a tall greenish drink. She handed the old man a beaker with a couple of inches of brandy in it. Her own drink looked like a Coke, straight. She sat down. Below the hem of the black skirt her legs were long and lovely and Sader caught himself staring at them.

"Ask her," suggested Ajoukian across his brandy beaker.

"Your husband received a telephone call at a bar around eleven o'clock on the night he dropped from sight. I wondered how the caller knew where to reach him, whether either you or his father—"

She cut in, "I had no idea where he went, once he left here."

"You knew his favorite places, I guess."

Her pink mouth pinched up as if with embarrassment. She turned her head to one side, the silver hair glowing as the light crossed it. "No. Not lately. We'd been—we'd had a little falling out." Her eyes stole over to the old man, then hurried on.

Sader said, "I don't think my partner knew that you and your husband were on the outs. That's a pretty important piece of information in a case of disappearance."

"Is it?" she asked, contrite.

"Had either of you thought about getting a divorce?"

"Oh, no."

The old man's harsh voice broke in. "It wouldn't have had anything to do with Perry's going away, if they had. He's in business with me, he wouldn't just walk out on what he had here." Ajoukian cast a fierce glance around, like a brigand totting up his spoils. "Women . . . any woman . . . wasn't worth that to him."

Mrs. Ajoukian looked at her father-in-law and he stared back. Sader got an impression of hatred, thinly concealed.

Then she murmured, "We still loved each other, Daddy," and Sader wondered if he had imagined the hostility.

The old man leaned forward from the blanket. "This is what you came to say, isn't it? You haven't found out a thing."

"What did you expect in the space of twenty-four hours?" Sader said.

"More than you've done."

The girl put in, "Mr. Sader, you're not drinking your drink. Isn't it what you like?"

"I'm a high-dive drinker," Sader told her. "That first taste of alcohol is the same as jumping off a ten-story building. I'd like to get back up, but I can't." He had put the greenish drink on the table by his chair. "So excuse me, and thanks anyhow."

"You're fired," said Ajoukian abruptly.

Sader looked into the black reptilian eyes. "I'll send my bill."

"I won't pay it." A funny color had come into the parchment skin, a reddish bloom that was far from the blush of health. The old man's mouth began to tremble. "Get out of here."

"Now, Daddy," cried the girl, springing up to run to him. "You've got to keep quiet. Dr. Bell told you to avoid any excitement."

"I won't pay you a cent," Ajoukian spat at Sader. "Throw him out, Connie. He's a fake."

She tried to smooth the shaking head, to pull the blanket around him. The old man struck at her with a clawlike hand. She looked over at Sader. "He's going to have one of his fits. He ought to be put in bed. I can't carry him. He drove off his nurse."

Sader walked to Ajoukian's chair, avoided a swipe of the hawk's claws, threw the blanket around the old man, and lifted him. She ran ahead, opening doors. They went down a carpeted hall past several rooms, into a big bedroom. She hurried to the bed, turned down the coverlets. Sader put Ajoukian into the lavender sheets, had his face raked in parting.

"Oh, I'm sorry! He got you, didn't he?" The velvety eyes seemed ready to weep velvet tears. She touched Sader's jaw with fingertips as cool as snow. On the bed, the old man was convulsed with coughing. "Wait here for just a moment, will you? I've got to telephone Dr. Bell."

Sader put a handkerchief to the welts on his cheek and sat down by the bed. "Mr. Ajoukian, a man was murdered today. His name was Mullens. He was a bookkeeper in a field office on Signal Hill. I think he knew something about the disappearance of Mrs. Wanderley. He might also have known something of the whereabouts of your son. Tell me —did this man contact you?"

The old man seemed torn by some terrible dilemma. His breathing had a broken, sucking sound like a pump thrown off beat. "Who's this fellow you're talking about?"

"You heard me."

"Mullens?" He seemed to sort hurriedly the clutter in his mind. "Well, maybe. Maybe."

"Maybe you went down to his office last night to meet him. Maybe that's when you caught your chill. There's a woman who saw you, who can identify you." Sader was convinced now that Tina Griffin had recognized that elderly man in the field office. That was why she'd kept harping on the clothes, the outward trappings, keeping off the subject of identity. She'd seen Ajoukian previously, of course, at Margot Cole's party, even though she may not have been introduced or have learned his name. Was she, like Mullens, trying to salvage something to sell?

A dangerous game. . . . Perhaps she hadn't wanted to make positive identification to spite Pettis. Or to keep herself from further questioning.

Ajoukian was whispering. "If Mullens is dead, it means he really did know something. Something more than . . ." The words died in a rattle. "It means my son is dead, perhaps." He turned his face, retreating into grief.

Mrs. Ajoukian came back. She bent above the old man. "Dr. Bell is coming right away."

"It doesn't matter now."

She threw a glance at Sader. "What have you told him?"

"There's been a murder. A man who may have known something of your husband's disappearance was killed this morning."

She seemed almost to stagger, her right ankle turning loosely. "Why should that happen?"

"My son is dead," said Ajoukian in his harsh broken whisper.

The room grew still. The girl's hands twisted, fumbled with her bracelets. "It isn't true, is it?"

"I don't know," said Sader. My best line, he thought grimly. In this affair I'm Johnny Know-Not. All I can find out is that there was a party, old man Ajoukian wanted to buy oil shares, and Mrs. Wanderley didn't like a job involving pigs. He walked to the door, turned back. "I hope I won't offend you, asking this. Was your husband interested in another woman?"

All at once old man Ajoukian sprang up in bed and roared, "Women! Women! Can't you get women out of your head for a minute? My son had money! He didn't have to worry over women!" Then he flopped back and lay wheezing.

The girl in the middle of the room flinched, turning from Sader. "If he had anyone, he'd met her recently. And perhaps, as Daddy says, it wouldn't have been serious."

Sader hated to leave her there. She was young and lovely, and her life under the thumb of the fierce old man couldn't be pleasant. He wondered what her marriage had been like, why she'd come to live here with her father-in-law and what sort of husband the son had been. Maybe Dan knew.

"I think your father-in-law had better get in touch with the police about the death of Mullens—when the doctor gives permission, of course."

"I'll see that he does."

"And you should call the Santa Ana sheriff's office, too."

She nodded obediently.

"Don't take anything for granted."

She smiled at his effort to cheer her, though the velvet eyes did not light up. She escorted him to the door. "Daddy didn't really mean to fire you."

"I'm not quitting whether he did or not. We're working on another disappearance. It seems to coincide oddly with that of your husband."

"Oh? And who is that?"

"A Mrs. Wanderley."

"She disappeared Tuesday night? When Perry did?"

"Not exactly. She was seen Wednesday morning." He saw the curiosity, and something like a touch of unwilling fear, in her glance. "I wish I could explain the connection. Let's just say it's a hunch."

"Who is she?"

"A well-to-do woman, came from an old Middle Western family, has a big house on Ocean Avenue, a daughter about your age."

She gave a husky breathless laugh. "You mean, an *old* woman?"

"Forty-seven," Sader said, feeling like a dinosaur. "Didn't look it. But I don't think your husband would have been attracted."

He expected her to be relieved, since he had thought her suspicions had been roused by the idea of some sort of elopement. But she shook her head as if mystified, a pinched expression settling on her lips. It seemed to Sader that all at once she had admitted to herself the things her husband had been—a chaser of women among others only she could know. "It's hard to say," she murmured. "It's hard to say just whom he might have liked." The words seemed dragged from her.

On this awkward note, Sader took his departure.

The rain had fined to a scattered, erratic sprinkling. He drove from Ajoukian's leafy lane to the highway, turned toward Long Beach. He switched on the radio, then clicked it off. At a service station on the edge of town he parked, went into the telephone booth, rang the office. Nobody answered. He tried the Wanderley house. Dan was there, apologetic about taking Miss Wanderley home. She'd looked lonely, he offered.

Sader, shut in the close stuffiness of the booth, seemed all at once to smell Kay's fresh perfume, and the memory of the way she'd turned to Dan tore through him. He knew how she'd look, looking lonely. "Sure," he said, "but you'd better start putting on the brakes. I think what you're experimenting with is polygamy, sort of."

"You met Mrs. Ajoukian?" Dan said, his voice suddenly warm.

"Still interested?"

"Oh, you know how it is."

Kay was within hearing distance, Sader judged. "I've got an idea for a job."

"Yours or mine?"

"Both. I want you to go over to San Pedro to a boat-supply shop and buy a couple of grappling hooks. Some rope. Check our flashlights."

The silence was long, drawn out, as if Dan had forgotten how to talk. Then he laughed unevenly and stammered, "Perish the thought—"

"Take a good look at Kay Wanderley," Sader said through his teeth. "She deserves a decent job done for her, not to have you hold her hand to console her. Get on it." He knew that Dan must sense the savage jealousy that stabbed him.

"Sure, Papa. Right away. Two grap—"

"Shut up." He rammed the phone into place and opened the booth.

CHAPTER ELEVEN

In the office Sader opened a drawer of Dan's desk and looked long at the rum bottle. Then he shut the drawer, went around to his own desk, and got a box of aspirin. He stepped into the outer office to draw a cup of water. He tossed two tablets into his mouth, washed them down, tasted the bitterness on the back of his tongue. The office was dark, the light almost gone, though it was scarcely five yet.

Dimly, his own reflection danced in the side of the water bottle. "What a clunk," he said to his distorted image. "Who do you think you're kidding? Dan's wise now." He wanted to jeer at himself, to poke fun; but something inside him was as heavy and cold and dead as a chunk of ice.

He went back into the other room where lights burned, sat down, typed up everything that had happened at the field office and later at the Ajoukians'. "We ought to invest in a tape recorder, a portable one," he said half aloud, imagining himself talking into one as he had driven toward Long Beach, saving all this work.

When he shut the office and went down to the street, the chimes of the big church on Pacific Avenue were ringing the half hour. It was half past six. He went over to Pine, turned left toward the beach. At the foot of Pine Avenue he walked down the incline to the beach, turned into the alley of garish light. The rain had stopped, though the skies had not cleared. There were knots of people, sailors mostly, strolling along the midway.

Milton's booth was lit and his pigs peered at Sader inquisitively from behind their wire netting. But Milton wasn't behind the counter urging the public to buy baseballs.

The man in the next concession, putting change into his change box, said, "Looking for Milt? He's in the bar yonder." He jerked a thumb at a flashing blue sign across the way.

A six-year-old kid with a wet taffy apple bumped into Sader. He was rubbing the stickiness with a handkerchief as he went into the bar. There were about a half dozen people on stools, a few more at tables. The light was poor and the jukebox thunderous. He picked out Milton Wanderley at a table in the back of the room, Tina Griffin with him, drinks on the table before them. They were watching him. Milton's sagging face was split in a smile. Tina's exotic, oriental eyes held a wary hurt as if she hoped Sader might go on out again.

He walked back. Milton half rose, brushing at his temple in the awkward gesture which was habitual. Sader said, "Mind if I join you for a minute?"

Milton beckoned the waitress. "What'll you have?"

"Coke," Sader told the girl. "Cold but no ice."

"Still on the wagon?" Tina bantered softly.

"Still on, but I don't know for how long," Sader said heavily. "A reformed drunk walks a tightrope every waking minute of his life."

"You used to drink, huh?" Milton asked.

"With enthusiasm." The Coke came and Sader tried it. Tina was shooting little glances at him, her slanted eyes enigmatic under her lashes. "I'm sorry about that incident on the Hill."

"I should be cross with you for making me go back."

"I didn't," Sader corrected without heat. "But I'm sorry anyway that Pettis treated you as he did. He wanted a confession from you."

"I knew that. I didn't have anything to confess." In the shadow of the silky black hair her brow was serene, unworried. Her long fingers on the glass she held betrayed no tremble of nervousness.

Milton must have heard from her of the murder in the field office. He said worriedly, "That guy's place is right below my house, not more than a half mile. I was home, I guess, when it happened. Is that what you came to ask me about?"

Sader said, "Just hoping you'd remember something."

"I was trying to sleep this morning. My head hurt, so after I'd fed and watered the pigs I took some sleeping pills and lay down with the blinds drawn. Sometimes it helps. Anyway, I had no idea anything was wrong down there. I'd never met this man Mullens. I live on the Hill because I get the house cheap and the landlord's away. I never did get acquainted with any of the oil people." He shifted on his chair. "How's it coming, looking for Felicia?"

"Nothing," said Sader, his lips tightening.

"What's Kay doing? Is she pretty upset?"

"The rain gets her."

"I see what you mean," Milton said, after considering it. "Anyone gone like that, perhaps something happened to them, you figure when the bad weather comes they might be out in it. Helpless. Dead, even. You think of them lying out all wet, no shelter, no warmth. Nobody to give a damn."

Tina shivered delicately. The jukebox switched to a new record and a cloying voice began to whisper of faithless love. Tina moved her glass, building a pattern of small close circles. "Where could she be? It couldn't be the Hill, there's no place to hide. Too many men work there. The place is full of people all day. They'd see her."

"I don't know," Milton argued. "If somebody was hurt, or dead, you could dump them lots of places. There's all kinds of gullies and holes, weed patches—"

"I've been wondering about that sump below Mullens's office." Sader watched them both, but nothing drifted across their faces except puzzlement, a mild surprise, and a touch of revulsion on Tina's part.

"They've fenced those things, what's left of them," Milton said. "Kids and dogs and cats used to fall in."

"What a horrible way to die. . . ." Tina said, strain in her voice.

Milton worried it around. "I'm always afraid those pigs of mine will get into oil, somehow. They can pry through a fence like weasels. One little hole, they'd be out, a line of follow-the-leader." He seemed eager now to lead the conversation away from Felicia. "I finally just moved them indoors. Maybe it wasn't an entirely honest thing—I didn't get the landlord's permission. He lives in San Bernardino, I just mail him the rent. I couldn't figure what else to do with the pigs."

"Quit worrying," Tina said. "You're always fretting over something. Why not just admit the pigs are company, and to hell with what anyone thinks?"

Sader remembered that he hadn't heard any disapproval of Milton from anyone, including the woman with the strange blue eyes, Margot Cole. Mrs. Cole had condemned Felicia Wanderley for her intolerance over Milton's pigs. He remembered too, now, the story of the party Monday night. He asked Tina, "Do you remember whether Charlie Ott and Ajoukian were at Mrs. Cole's party at the same time?"

It caught her off guard and her reply stumbled. "Ajoukian?"

Sader's glance was ironic, mocking; and she saw it and color came into her face. "An elderly man. Very well dressed, I imagine. You can always tell good tailoring. You saw Felicia Wanderley there, of course."

She nodded mutely. Milton broke in with, "Have you figured what she was mad about at my place? Somebody not being honest, or something like that?"

"I have a couple of leads," Sader answered. To himself he admitted their uncertain quality. No one could say definitely that Felicia Wanderley had been angry about Ajoukian's proposal to buy Margot Cole's oil shares. Mrs. Cole had reasons for not co-operating. Ajoukian wouldn't discuss his business affairs.

Charlie Ott might have been sabotaging Mrs. Wanderley in regard to her fee for selling his duplex. He wasn't talking, any more than was Mrs. Cole or Ajoukian.

"I guess," Sader corrected somberly, "I should say I have a couple of hunches."

Milton fiddled with his drink. "I wish I could help you. I wish I'd seen something this morning. But gosh, I didn't even know the guy down there in the office was in danger. I still don't see how his murder ties in with Felicia."

Tina brushed at a wing of hair that had fallen along her cheek. The oriental look had deepened around her eyes, so that Sader seemed to see a mask chiseled with a tool, remote and haughty. "No one's proved it has," she said softly.

Sader thought about the oil sump and Dan's errand to buy the grappling hooks. The cold, dead feeling grew heavier; and he wished he could have had a drink. One drink.

"My God, does it have to rain forever?" Dan got out of the car and looked at the dark and shuddered. They were parked in the lee of the office where Mullens had died. In the black sky overhead Sader sensed clouds, wet and heavy, rolling along like a fleet of overloaded trucks. Dan pulled ropes and grappling hooks from the floor of the back seat. "On a night like this a man should go to bed with a good book. Remind me, Papa. Next time it's like this and you pull me out into the weather, I'm resigning."

"Didn't you wear your rubbers, sonny?" Sader asked, pretending to worry about it. "Need your nose wiped?" He tested the big flashlight; its beam cut across the weedy slope, showed the wet earth, and struck silver in the falling rain. Off in the distance a few lights blinked where rigs were working. The town was blotted out in the storm.

"When I need my nose wiped I'll ask for prettier hands than yours," Dan jeered, then waited to see what Sader would reply. "That Kay Wanderley's a cute mouse. I wouldn't mind some attention from her."

Sader knew his partner was baiting him and kept silent. They walked down the slope from the office, came to the embankment and the fence surrounding the oil sump.

"You know what we'll get out of here, don't you?" Dan shuffled, the iron hooks clanged together. "Twenty-two dead cats. Old tires. Some old love letters preserved in asphalt."

Sader didn't answer. He went over to the gate and put the light on the lock, and then said something in a low voice.

"Something wrong?" Dan asked.

"New lock today," Sader answered.

"It's not very high. We can climb it." He proved this by putting a hand on the top bar of the gate and vaulting over.

Sader went over by pulling himself up, squirming across, dropping on the other side. He felt Dan standing off in the dark watching him. "I hate show-offs," he said. Dan laughed cruelly, and Sader flushed, thankful that the light wasn't on him and Dan couldn't see.

They went up the embankment and Sader flicked the beam of light around over the surface of the oil. There were still bubbles out in the middle. He pointed them out to Dan. "Let's aim for them."

Dan went on complaining about the rain all the time they cast and drew in. Until the third try. That was when he got the handbag.

"First bundle of old love letters," Dan said, as the hook dragged up out of the ooze and he saw something trailing. Then Sader came over and put the light on it, and they saw what it was. "Oh, oh. This is what happens when the purse snatchers get through with them."

Sader squatted, took out a handkerchief, wiped the clinging oil from the bag. Rain spattered on the leather as he cleaned it. "Hold the light." He twisted the catch and pulled the purse open. Purse and contents were sodden, permeated with oil. Some paper fell to pieces as Sader lifted it forth. Cigarettes, a book of matches, and some other stuff was welded together, black with oil, oozing a thin stained stream of water. He found a leather wallet.

He stood up, opened the wallet, wiped at the plastic compartments. Dan stood at his shoulder with the light.

"She let her driver's license expire," Dan said finally.

"She lopped seven years off her age, too," Sader added. He flipped open the money compartment. Soaked bills shone with a greasy slime. "Not robbed, at any rate."

"Maybe worse. You going to fish some more, huh?"

Sader grunted, put the wallet on top of the purse. Dan laid the light down on the bank so that it illuminated the pool. They went back to work. After about ten minutes, Sader said, "We aren't getting out into the middle."

"You figure she could crawl there after she was tossed in?"

"There's always water on the bottom of the sump,"

Sader told Dan. "A body would gravitate to the lowest spot. Probably out farther than we're hitting it."

Dan took off his slicker. "Watch this, Papa." He heaved, and the line went far out and the hook dropped into the black surface. He started to pull in, then stopped. "Caught on an old tree trunk." His teeth were white in the reflected light as he grinned at Sader, down the bank.

Sader walked back and they pulled together. The thing on the hook bobbed to the surface just in front of their feet, and Dan yelped. Sader let the line slacken, and cursed.

They waited for a minute. Dan's breath was harsh and whistling, and Sader thought he could hear his teeth chatter. "What do you think it is?" Dan asked. "Is it—her?"

"Could be. Could be anybody."

"Suppose we dig up some perfect stranger? Couldn't we just leave him here and go home?" Dan tried to laugh, but the sound was hollow. "After all, we've got Mrs. Wanderley's handbag. We could work on that for a while."

"This is the place where the boys get off the line and the men go on to the station," Sader said grimly. "You going or staying?"

"God damn you, who you calling yellow?" Dan went on to curse Sader thoroughly, and betrayed his popping nerves. Sader listened for a couple of minutes, the rope slack in his hands, and then suddenly he snapped at Dan to shut up and get to work. They pulled the thing from the oil, up to the top of the bank.

"It's a man!" Dan bent over the figure. He'd picked up the flashlight, trained the beam on the body. The stench of oil seemed suddenly stronger in the damp night air. The hook was embedded in the clothing at the waist. The coat had dragged half off the arms and the body lay on its face. With a grimace, Sader knelt and pushed at the inert shoulder. Dan backed away.

"Keep the light still, damn you."

"Sure, Papa. He needs his face washed. What'll we call him?"

Sader's handkerchief, already soaked with oil from cleaning the purse, didn't make much impression on the gummy stuff that clung to the features of the dead man. "Give me something. The tail of your shirt. Or your raincoat. I've got to have a look at him."

"Use your own shirt." But grudgingly, Dan held out a clean handkerchief. "I'm going to put this on the expense account. Pure linen. My aunt bought me a dozen for Christmas, a dollar apiece."

"You never had a dollar handkerchief in your life." Sader worked over the dead man, averting his face as much as possible from the stench of oil. "Black hair. A young guy. Heavy brows, full lips. No telling what color the eyes were." He shrugged and stood up, dropping Dan's handkerchief on the body. "I can't do any more with him. We need a telephone."

"Aren't you going to make an identification?"

"I can't. I think it's young Ajoukian. His wife will be brought in and asked to identify him. They'd better leave the old man alone. He's sick."

"Him and me too," Dan growled.

"Wait here, will you? I'll try to get into that office to use the phone. If I can't get in I'll have to drive over to Cherry."

"Let me go."

Sader didn't smile, but his tone was dry, amused. "Sure. Run along."

Again Dan erupted into curses. "You think you're so damned tough, so goddam smart. I ought to belt you one for insulting me."

Sader took out cigarettes and matches and proceeded to light up. Dan walked around a little.

"I didn't mean it, Red."

"You're just nervous," Sader jeered. "You can leap over fences like Tarzan, but a dead guy in a sump unlaces you."

"Yeah, yeah. Rub it in. Feel good. Get a big head over it. Make love to the Wanderley babe. Tell her how wonderful you are."

"Are you going to wait here while I telephone?"

"This guy and I are going to have a crap game," Dan said. "We'll be real sociable. I might win all of his money. Speaking of money, why don't you look in his clothes for his wallet?"

"You can do that while I'm telephoning." Sader went back to the gate, crawled over, lighted his way to the office where he found a rear window unlocked. When he had located Pettis and talked to him, he walked back to the sump. Dan was using his flashlight now, but not on the body. He was shining it aimlessly out over the oil sump, whistling to himself in the lonely dark.

He came down to the gate, leaned there, waiting for Sader. "It's Ajoukian, all right. You want to know how I figure it? Mrs. Wanderley was sore because old Ajoukian was buying the oil shares from her friend, taking advantage of a woman in trouble. The son comes out to reason with her. She's all lit up. To cool her down, he suggests a walk. She ups and murders him. Somehow, tossing in the body, her purse tangles and goes along. Then, getting worried, she arranges that scene with the cab driver to draw attention from her presence here on the Hill."

Sader leaned against the other side of the gate, lit a new cigarette from the old one, listened to the pumps chuckling in the distance. "We might stack it up that way when we get a few more answers. Who called young Ajoukian at the bar? Where did she get ammo for the gun? Who fell into those vines by the office door? And where is Felicia Wanderley now?"

"Aaah, they're just minor details," Dan assured him.

CHAPTER TWELVE

The lane was dark, Ajoukian's lights glowing at the end. Sader parked in the drive, went to the door, rang the faraway chiming bells. It was some time before the door opened. A gray-haired woman in a white nurse's uniform looked out at him. "Yes, sir?"

"Is Mrs. Ajoukian in?"

"She should have answered the bell," the nurse said. "I'll go see, though. Whom shall I say is here?"

"Sader."

She went away, her rubber heels smacking the tiled floor of the hall. The smell of the indoor greenery stole out, a wet damp hot-house odor that contrasted with the rainy night, and Sader wrinkled his nose. He tried to pre-phrase his message for Ajoukian's beautiful young widow. The police would like to see her at the morgue. Or perhaps, if she could give them the name of a family friend who could identify her husband, they'd accept that temporarily. Until she stopped crying, perhaps. Sometimes widows broke down and had hysterics, or even fainted. Pettis's aversion for such actions had been thinly hidden under the request for Sader to bring the news to the family. He'd tried to imply that since Sader was grossly overpaid hired help, he might as well earn some small part of his money.

The nurse came back, looking busy and indifferent. "She isn't here."

"It's very important that I talk to her or to Mr. Ajoukian."

"Mr. Ajoukian isn't at all well. He had a heart attack late this afternoon. Maybe I could take a message for him."

"They found the body of his son tonight."

She looked so shocked that Sader knew she'd been unaware of the son's disappearance. "Oh, dear!" She wavered in indecision, then added, "I'll call the doctor. Perhaps you could see Mr. Ajoukian for a minute." She rushed off again.

This time she came back quickly, shaking her head. "I'm sorry. Dr. Bell doesn't want Mr. Ajoukian to be told of his son's death until he can see him again tomorrow." She eyed Sader curiously. "Was it an accident?"

"His son's been missing several days. I don't think they know yet what killed him." He nodded good-bye and walked away. He was in his car, his fingers on the key in the switch, when headlights turned in at the other end of the lane, crept toward the house. He waited. The other car stopped at the edge of the drive, a door slammed, quick steps crunched in the gravel. Sader opened his door again and got out.

The lights behind her lit up Mrs. Ajoukian's silver hair like a halo. She peered toward him. "Mr. Sader? You've brought news?"

"Bad news, I'm afraid."

She seemed to fall crookedly against the side of her fender. He sprang to catch her, but she said breathlessly, "I turned my foot on a stone. Have you told Daddy?"

"The doctor wouldn't give permission."

Her head bent; she seemed to collect herself. "He had a bad day. After you went he had a crying fit, and then coughed a lot, and finally went into a sort of convulsion. Dr. Bell said his heart is weak. We found another nurse." The rain was settling in the silver hair, on the shoulders of her fur coat. "Is—is Perry dead?"

"Yes."

"Did you find him?"

"We found his body in an oil sump. The police want you to identify him if you feel up to it. Otherwise, a family friend will do."

She stumbled back to the door of her car, cut the switch on the motor and killed the lights, came back to him in the dark. He smelled the perfume she wore, dry and winy. Her hand touched his, the cool fingers clinging. "Let's go in and sit down. You tell me more, then."

There was a fire in the enormous fireplace—not very big; it looked lost in the cavern of brick. She shed the fur coat on a checkered lounge and walked to the fire and looked at it somberly. "It doesn't seem possible. I can't believe he's dead. He had a kind of—well, animal vitality is the way I thought of it. Like a gorilla. Invincible."

She didn't sound as if she'd loved the gorilla overly much, Sader thought, but you never could tell. He was surprised at the lack of reaction in her. It seemed to be a mask, covering shock perhaps. She turned around to look at Sader. In that moment he decided that she was the most beautiful woman he'd ever seen. There wasn't a flaw in the soft face, the silver curls, the slim figure dressed in red wool. Almost too perfect, he added to himself, to be real. A doll that had learned to talk, to move, to understand. A doll with a steel spring instead of a heart.

No, that wasn't being fair to her. "Do you want me to call someone to identify your husband?"

"I'll go." Her tone was quiet and composed. "Let me think for a little bit, and get warm." She pushed aside the coat on the checkered couch and sat down, pointed to a chair for Sader. "How did Perry die?"

"I saw what looked to be a gunshot wound over his temple. But there was so much oil on him, too—don't take it as final."

"Do you think he's been dead ever since he went away?"

"Only a postmortem would give that information. And maybe even then not definitely. Personally, I think he died shortly after eleven o'clock on Tuesday night."

The big brown eyes grew puzzled. "Why are you so sure?"

"I think the person who called him at the barbecue bar is the last person who saw him alive." He turned away from that other conviction, for Kay's sake, that Mrs. Wanderley had used the gun.

"Why should anyone *want* to murder my husband?" The firelight on the silver curls dappled them with gold. "He was young, a little ruthless, maybe. But what had he done, that he should be killed?" She seemed so intent on his answer that Sader was almost embarrassed.

"Can't you supply that information?"

She averted her face. The fire painted a golden line on her profile. "I guess—sometimes a wife is the last to know. If there *was* anything—"

"Well, perhaps you'd quarreled—"

She shook her head. "Not over women. Please don't think that. It was about money. The old man thought I spent too much. Perry tried to keep the peace." She looked at Sader, the brown eyes velvety in regret. "Ask him, ask Mr. Ajoukian."

Well, Sader thought, she's stopped calling him Daddy. He studied the huge, luxurious room. He wondered how much of this would be claimed by the widow. If she had no claim here, where would she go; what would she do?

Perhaps Sader's interest in the house displeased her subtly. She rose, lifted the coat. "Where do we go to see about Perry?" For just an instant he imagined a catch in her voice—had it been real?—and he wondered if under the gorgeous surface there lurked grief he couldn't even imagine, whether inwardly she could be lost, terrified. He stepped over to help her with the coat. "Did you talk to Mr. Ajoukian tonight?"

"No."

"I'd better speak to the nurse before I leave. Can you let yourself out?"

"Don't worry about me. I'll be out beside the cars."

She hesitated, looking back at the warm hearth as though envying the comfort of that spot. Was she thinking just then of the cold depths of the sump? Apparently not—

"We'll go in my car," she said, touching his hand with her cool fingers. "When we get home again, I'll write a check for you."

It was a funny time to think about settling his account. "There's no hurry. You can mail it anytime."

"Please come back with me." She moved over to the door as if embarrassed that she should have to beg for his company at such a time. There was nothing Sader could do but to agree, though he had wanted to be with Kay Wanderley when the police interviewed her about her mother's handbag.

At twelve-fifteen Sader went back to the Pike. It had been a quiet night because of the bad weather; most of the concessions were closed. In Milton's booth, however, lights burned and the little pigs still peered from behind the wire netting. Sader walked over to an open-front café where the cook at the griddle stood facing the traffic. The smell of coffee and fried hamburgers and fish and chips drowned out the rainy tang on the night air. "Do you know Milton, the guy with the pigs?"

The cook flipped a couple of meat patties. "Yeah. He's around somewhere. Saw him tonight."

Sader went to the bar, but Milton wasn't in it. Finally he returned to the booth, hopped the counter, and investigated the space behind the pigs. It was a crudely boarded-in closet, the width of the room, perhaps four feet deep, furnished with some sacks of feed, a tottering card table, and an army cot. Milton lay on the cot, his face turned to the bare bulb that burned in the ceiling. He was asleep with his mouth open.

Sader shook him awake. "You're wanted at police head-quarters on the Hill."

"About that dead guy at the field office?" Milton said, after yawning himself awake. He bent to put on his shoes. "I don't know anything about him."

"New client this time. There was a dead man in the sump. They want you to look him over."

Milton went on lacing his sneakers, his fingers awkward with the ties. He kept his head down. "I still don't know anything. Why can't they leave me alone? Next thing you know, they'll jump on me for keeping my pigs in the house."

"Couldn't your pigs stay down here for one night?"

"You crazy?" Milton shot him an angry look from below. "There's no way to lock this place good. I got to take my prizes and the pigs home every night. Wouldn't be nothing left here in the morning."

"I'll tell you what I'll do," Sader said. "You run up there and talk to the cops and I'll stay here with your pigs and merchandise."

The offer seemed to surprise Milton. "You will?"

"Sure. I've been almost everything else. Let me be a pig sitter once in my life."

"It's good of you to offer." Milton seemed to turn Sader's generosity over in his mind, as if seeking something ulterior in it. "I couldn't pay you for it, though. I know your time's worth money."

"This is on me," Sader told him.

Milton picked a leather jacket up off the broken table, nodded to Sader and went out. The narrow room grew quiet except for the minor trottings of the pigs in their cages. Once in a while he could catch the singsong chant of the cook in the open-front café, the invitation to dine having about as much relation to normal speech as the hamburgers had to ordinary food. Sader picked around through the magazines and comics Milton had on the floor at the head of the cot. He decided that Milton liked stories about space men with antennas on their heads who were thwarted by earth heroes. He noted the presence, in these yarns, of lovely young ladies in danger of being carried off to set up housekeeping on Mars. This could mean that Milton had a subconscious compulsion about being a hero. It could even mean, Sader thought wistfully, that Milton had shot young Ajoukian because in the heat of an argument he thought Ajoukian was threatening Mrs. Wanderley. This was interesting.

Even more interesting was Milton's lack of curiosity about the identity of the man in the sump.

Sader sat on the army cot and lit cigarettes one after another. He thought about Milton, Milton's possible motives as a murderer; but in dealing with the Wanderley cousin he knew he had to allow for certain deviations from normal behavior because of Milton's head injury. It would be hard to be logical and consistent with a steady throb in your brain.

The pigs seemed restless, so Sader went over and looked into the back doors of their pens, and filled their water cups from a faucet in the corner, and gave them some of the grain in the sacks. They regarded him with eager affection and ignored the corn. Sader decided they were already full, had only craved attention. He was returning the metal scoop to the open bag of grain when he heard a noise at the back door. Someone had rapped faintly on the panel.

Sader walked to the other end of the narrow space, turned the key, pulled the door inward. The row of concessions backed up to the side of the pier at this point. There was a promenade of a few feet in width, then the pier railing, the sea beyond. The light wasn't too good, but Sader made out the figure of a woman in a dark coat and hat. It was a moment before he recognized her, before the strange blue eyes under the hat brim registered and brought back her name. Margot Cole.

"I'm looking for Milton," she said, and her tone showed that she had not as yet recognized Sader. She tried to peer past him into the room. Over her temples her hair was pulled tight as he remembered it and the heavy bun on her neck distorted the line of the brim. "Isn't he here?"

"Come in," Sader invited, stepping back. She looked at him quickly, knowing him now. "Milton's out on an errand."

She came in, turned swiftly to face him. "The police have been to my house. I think you must have suggested that they come there and question me. I've been trying quietly to work out a reconciliation with my husband. That's ruined now. He's leaving." Sader recalled the quiet steps he'd heard in Margot Cole's house, her secretive attitude. "None of my friends liked him, but I was willing to give them up. Now the police have barged in, asking about Ajoukian and his business, and my husband knows I was trying to raise money. It wasn't really for a divorce, though I told you so; and it's what my husband believes."

She was shaking with anger, her heavy face taut with

repressed hatred and indignation. Sader thought, remembering her calm demeanor in her home, that she was probably a woman slow to rouse to rage; but once roused she'd hold a grudge forever.

Sader tried to explain. "I didn't have any choice. There has to be a connection between young Ajoukian and Mrs. Wanderley—her purse was with his body in that sump. But the only link I can find was the meeting between Ajoukian's father and Mrs. Wanderley at your house Monday night."

She stuck her face up close to his. He felt the heat of her breath. She'd had a drink recently—perhaps after the police had gone, after her husband had denounced her for perfidy. "There has to be another way! She exchanged only a few words with the old man."

"He says she wanted to know what he was doing there."

Mrs. Cole stamped her foot hard. "She wouldn't kill a man over his wanting to buy my oil shares! It's the craziest idea I've ever heard of! That's why I came to see Milton. He lives right above that oil sump. He must know what happened down there!"

"He says he doesn't."

She walked to the army cot and sat down on it. "I'll get it out of him."

"You're going to wait for him?"

She looked at Sader with loathing. "As much as I hate being in the same room with you—yes."

"I'll leave, then." Sader went over to the other door, the one that led to the front of the concession. The pigs oinked lonesomely at him. "Milton wanted someone to stay here until he got back. I was just watching his stuff. Goodnight, Mrs. Cole."

She bared her teeth at him in a grimace that had no resemblance to a parting smile. With this catlike farewell fresh in his mind, Sader crossed the Pike to the bar and used the telephone to ring his office. He had expected Dan to have gone home by now, and was surprised when Dan answered his call. "Tell me about Kay Wanderley."

"Papa, I hate to say this, but she blames you."

"Were you with her when the police showed her the handbag?"

"Yeah, I was right there all the time. She wants a lawyer now. I guess we're out of two jobs."

Sader's forehead wrinkled; he ran a hand across the stubby, red-gray hair, and it sprang back like mown wheat under the scythe. "I've got to see her."

"She won't let you in that big house any more. I think she expected us to keep that handbag to ourselves."

"I'm going out there anyway."

Sader hurried back to the lot where he kept his car, drove out Ocean Avenue to Scotland Place. There was no rain now. The big avenue was wide and empty. He saw no lights in the Wanderley house, but rang the bell anyway. He figured she'd send Annie down to drive him away with a scathing tongue; but instead, when the door opened, there was Kay. She was so exactly the image he'd carried all day, that for an instant he couldn't speak.

She hesitated, then said formally, "It's too late, Mr. Sader, to ask you in."

"I know. I'd be intruding, according to my partner. I just came to ask you a question."

The big solemn gray eyes were steady on his. "What is the question?"

He put a hand on the doorframe as if to brace himself. "Something I haven't figured out yet. Miss Wanderley— what happened to your dog?"

CHAPTER THIRTEEN

She moved swiftly to slam the door, then must have seen his fingers curled around the doorframe. There was an instant, he thought, in which she would have liked to cut him across the knuckles; but she'd had a good bringing-up, and she controlled the desire for mayhem. "Wh—what did you say?"

"The dog," he reminded quietly. "Your mother wrote down an appointment for getting a dog license; and you said you had checked and she had been at the animal shelter when she was supposed to be. Only it occurs to me that I haven't seen any dog. You do let it inside, don't you, when it rains?"

There was a light behind her in the hall, but her face was shadowed. He couldn't judge what she went through just then. Probably some instinct urged her to protect her mother's reputation, and she already hated him for leaving the handbag with dead young Ajoukian. There was no doubt but that she was frightened and despairing. "Will you come inside?"

"I don't have to. Just answer that one query, and I'll go."

"I . . . I can't answer with a couple of words. The little dog is dead. There's more to it than—just that."

"How much more?"

She bent her face into her cupped hand; her voice came muffled. "I'll tell you the whole story if you come inside. I don't want to disturb Annie. She might hear us. Her room's right over our heads."

Sader thought of Annie's rigid propriety and walked softly. He went with Kay to the living room. It was cool in there as if the heat had been turned off hours ago, and the only smells were those of wax and polish. All the fine furniture had been placed chummily as if at any moment some very exclusive guests might want to come in and sit down—Annie's doing, Sader thought. She wouldn't like it if she were down here now and saw him sitting in a chair fixed for somebody who was somebody. He knew suddenly that he never came into this room without realizing that the city in which he had grown up had a side to it he had never known.

Kay Wanderley was dressed in a loose-fitting pique housecoat, bright ruby red that made her skin look white as cream. Her hair fell loose on her shoulders. She sat down and put her knees together, rubbed her hands over them, and said, "I found Tootsie early Wednesday morning. She was lying at the door, on the terrace." Kay's glance flickered over to the terrace entry. "I rushed her to a veterinarian. He said she was dead, that she'd been beaten, her skull crushed. I—I did a kind of crazy thing. I brought her home and tried to keep her warm in some blankets. I wouldn't believe she was . . . gone."

Sader began to light a cigarette. "Did your mother ever get mad at the dog when she was drinking?"

Kay nodded, her mouth pinched and trembling. "Yes. Tootsie annoyed Mother then. If she knew I wanted Mother to stay home, she'd try to keep her here."

"So you figured your mother had killed the dog in a rage."

The strain showed in Kay's voice, suddenly thin, frightened. "I'm sure Mother wouldn't intentionally harm the least creature. Your attitude about Mother has been wrong from the beginning. You've thought of her as an old . . . an old witch. . . ." She turned her face from him, unwilling for him to see her tears. When she could speak again, she went on. "What Mother was—I've told you. She had a world that she loved and it fell apart, and then she was lost. She was like a child alone in the dark."

Sader looked at her, musing on the fact that Kay, who was so young, should feel so much pity for the aging, rebellious mother. She was an unusual daughter. Or, more likely, Mrs. Wanderley had been explicit about the things which had driven her to drink. He asked, "Was the dog out on the swing when I came here?"

Kay nodded. "Yes. After you left I called the pound and they came and got the body."

"Then it was yesterday that you made up your mind the dog couldn't be wished back to life. And perhaps you admitted finally to yourself that your mother might have killed the pet because it tried to keep her from leaving while you were calling to her to stay. You must have decided that your mother's mood was more dangerous than you had guessed. That scared you." He saw the flinching motion of her shoulders. "Where was Annie all this time?"

"She'd gone to bed early. I woke her when Mother ran out with the gun, and she put on a robe and looked out into the street and couldn't see anyone. Afterward I decided Mother must have left by way of the terrace. That's where she would have run into Tootsie, who might have tried to stop her by catching hold of her coat. Probably Mother took a swing at Tootsie, not really meaning—not even knowing —she'd hurt her."

Sader grunted. "Well, I would have appreciated knowing about the dog and the gun at the beginning."

"It doesn't matter now, does it? The police have already convicted Mother of killing this young man, Ajoukian, and the other man in the office." Kay's hands twisted together on the lap of the red housecoat, her knuckles pulled white. "They've got it all figured out so neatly. Only—wait and see—it didn't happen that way."

The ringing of the telephone cut across her words. She hurried out, came back immediately. "The call is for you, Mr. Sader." Sader gave her a crooked grin; she averted her eyes. "Use the phone in the reception nook at the end of the hall. It's private there." She sat down stiffly and crossed her ankles.

Dan was on the line, his voice thick, rattling words off in excitement. "My God, Papa, you've got news for the Wanderley babe! Her mother didn't kill young Ajoukian. She's innocent, in the clear like a bird."

Sader said uneasily, "They've caught the murderer?"

"No. They found her. Right in that same sump we fished Ajoukian out of. What do you think of that?"

If Dan had been there, Sader would have hit him. As it was, the phone hung in his hand and he looked at the wall, while heat ran across his skin and the tendons twitched in his wrists. Finally he said dully, "What's the set-up?"

"Both of them shot with a twenty-two, Pettis thinks. The cops are draining the sump to find the gun. They want Kay Wanderley back up here. They're going after the Cole woman again, too."

"She's with Milton Wanderley."

"Milton's up here, having fits over his cousin."

"Tell them I left Margot Cole waiting for Milton in his pig concession." Sader hung up the phone and went down the hall to the living room and looked through the open door at the girl across the room. The red color of her housecoat seemed to swim up the wall like a flash of fire. He rubbed his eyes.

She looked up at him when he got close to her. "This you've got to believe: the purse there in the oil sump doesn't mean Mother killed him." She might as well have been speaking a foreign language; Sader just stared blankly. "Didn't you hear me?"

He sat down in front of her on the chair that should have been holding someone important, and said, "They've just found your mother. You don't owe me a thing. I didn't complete the job." He drew in his breath, a big breath that never seemed to end. He wanted to yawn, a reflex from strain.

"What did you say?"

He tried to imagine what had made him say the crazy thing about the fee. It was no time to think of money. It was a time to get across to her, gently but firmly, that she didn't have to worry any more about her mother being out in the rain. Her mother had been waterproofed. He said slowly, "I wish this job were anyone's but mine. They took your mother from the oil sump where we found Ajoukian earlier tonight."

Her hands quivered on the arms of her chair. Her eyes didn't falter but something new came into them, a depth of horror and outrage that stunned Sader. He said, "Shall I call Annie?"

He had to repeat the question before she replied. Then she said, "No. Don't call her. I want to go up there. There must be some mistake."

His mind cringed away from the sight that awaited her. He argued briefly. She told him, "Wait here. I'm going to get dressed."

While she was out of the room, Sader walked around in it and looked at the nice well-dusted furniture and the subdued modern pictures on the walls and listened to the sudden burst of rain against the terrace doors. Out there in the rainy dark were the gay canvas chairs, the big swing, abandoned to the weather because the mistress of the house was dead.

He thought about Mrs. Wanderley, who had been the transplanted fruit of an old purse-proud Middle Western family, and who had reigned in a regulated society and in an ordered household like a queen. Some unpleasant things had happened to her. Her husband had died, she'd been lonely; and the town had been gorged by a new population to whom she hadn't been anyone of importance. So she'd taken to drink and to rages she couldn't control.

Still, he thought, the same widowhood, the same change in neighbors, must have overtaken many another middle-aged woman in the town. And most would seem to have adjusted, somehow. The facts spoke of a deep flaw in Mrs. Wanderley, a delayed adolescent craving for flattery and attention. Her reaction to changing times had been infantile in its greed, its lack of consideration for her child.

He thought of Kay, upstairs now, hurrying into her clothes, convinced that there was some mistake, that it couldn't be her mother in the dregs of an old oil sump, stained and smeared and bloated, stinking. Sader beat a fist into his palm, over and over, trying to think of some way to keep her here. Give them time to clean the body, to take away the stench and the smear. Give Kay a few hours to gain composure.

Resolve hardened in him when he heard her quick steps in the hall.

She came in dressed in the neat blue wool dress, the fur jacket, the little velvet cap, which she had worn at the office. Under the small brim her hair was ragged. She'd made no attempt to put on makeup. "Shall we go?"

In her voice he heard the trembling of panic. "I guess so." He walked toward her. "I could make an excuse for you, delay this awhile."

"It isn't necessary." She waited for him, clutching her handbag, her face lifted a little as if that were the only way to keep her chin steady.

Sader nodded. "Keep the pose, please." His fist came up in a short clipping blow that spun her head back. Her eyes were already glassy as she started to fold at the knees. Sader caught her. He held her at the waist and stripped off the hat and the jacket, dropped them to the floor, swung Kay up into his arms and headed for the hall. He went upstairs where he kicked on doors until Annie opened one.

The gray mouse looked ready to fight. "What're you doing with her?" She sprang at him with claws.

"Smooth down. She wanted to see her mother's body. I clipped her one. Show me where to put her. And keep her here, at least until morning."

Annie seemed ready to faint with shock and outrage. Then she slowly wobbled off up the hall. She had on a kind of nightgown that Sader would have sworn, offhand, hadn't been sold since around 1890. Probably she sewed the atrocities at home in the room downstairs; certainly such objects were on display nowhere. She opened a bedroom door, swept through, turned down the covers of a wide white bed, stood glaring as if expecting some indecent trickery on his part. Sader put Kay down gently. Annie fussed over the girl, removed her shoes and loosened her collar. "How do I know you haven't killed her?"

Sader replied, "She's breathing. When she comes to, put an ice bag on her jaw, and give her some aspirin."

He started out. Annie ran after him, her gown dragging around her toes. "Where did they find Mrs. Wanderley?"

"In an old oil sump on Signal Hill."

Annie muttered distractedly under her breath, then gathered her wits to ask, "How long has she been dead?"

"I don't know." Striding down the hall, he was engrossed briefly with the puzzle. It seemed logical to think that Mrs. Wanderley and young Ajoukian had died together. She had been seen alive after dawn on Wednesday. How could the two have been murdered by daylight, thrown into the open sump without notice except from Mullens? And then an additional point nagged him. Mullens hadn't seemed sufficiently dismayed to be hiding a double killing. Sader's gaze grew bleak. At any rate, one thing was true. As Dan had said, Mrs. Wanderley had been cleared of the suspicion of murder—drunk, bad-tempered, or whatever, notwithstanding.

At the top of the stairs Annie plucked at his sleeve. "You took a lot on yourself, doing what you did just now."

"Yes, I guess I did."

"Well, no doubt you meant to save her a shock. I like a man who can act quickly. By the way, I have something to tell you." She cocked her head, measuring him, perhaps trying to see if he deserved this confidence. "I overheard a telephone conversation of Mrs. Wanderley's on the night she left here."

The bleakness in Sader didn't diminish. "This might have helped, sooner."

"You know my position is a subordinate one in this household," she said, watching him to see if he believed it. "A proper servant must keep her mouth shut. A gabbling maid is a curse to her calling."

"My experience is so limited," Sader complained.

She pursed her lips. "Mrs. Wanderley wanted to find someone named Ajoukian."

"I gather you've read the late papers?"

"I subscribe to the London *Times* and to *Punch*," she lectured gently. "They get here a bit late. The American press is so sensational and so full of politics."

"You're a funny little gal. Anyway, a young guy named Ajoukian was in the sump, dead, along with Mrs. Wanderley. She was sleeping, you might say, with a stranger. Or I had thought him a stranger until now. What did she want of Mr. Ajoukian?"

"She was quarreling with him, finally."

"What about?"

Annie hesitated. "She wasn't very coherent. At one point, though, I heard her mention Mr. Ott's name. You know, the rather large seedy gentleman she'd known so long. She said something like, 'I know Charlie Ott is mixed up in this somewhere.' At this point I tactfully moved out of hearing."

"It was the wrong time for tact."

Annie's glance implied that he lacked a sense of decency. "I didn't intentionally hear what I did."

Sader put a hand on the newel post, gazed thoughtfully down at the space below. "Charlie Ott. A very interesting fellow."

Annie withheld comment. She'd called Ott a gentleman, but Sader sensed that this was a term loosely applied.

"Miss Wanderley has told me that when her mother left here Tuesday night, she was waving a gun and threatening to go 'up there'—presumably to the Hill—and scare some unnamed character out of his wits. Would it have been logical for that character to have been Charlie Ott?" Sader put the question, then waited while Annie appeared to be figuring something in her head.

"Of course, Miss Wanderley told me the same thing," Annie said carefully. "And I saw no reason to doubt this. But at the same time, I can't quite believe that her mother's anger over the business which concerned Mr. Ajoukian was murderous in its intensity."

"Perhaps she thought of something more, some other transaction which involved Ott."

Annie's glance was cautious. "Of course it's true, she had a contract with him to sell his property."

"It's what I was thinking of," Sader told her.

"I can't help you. I was in bed by the time she left. Miss Wanderley roused me to help her find her mother and keep her at home. I didn't see Mrs. Wanderley at that time."

Sader went down a couple of steps, then looked back at Annie. "Did you like her?"

There was no wavering in Annie's gaze. "Very much." She added nothing; her glance was chiding. Sader decided that he was expected to know why she had been devoted to Mrs. Wanderley. Well, he thought, perhaps he did, at that. Mrs. Wanderley must have shown her careful breeding in her sober moments. The patina left by wealth, security, and family pride wouldn't have worn off quickly. He knew nothing of a life with servants but some instinct told him that Felicia Wanderley would have exploited the motherly instincts of this small gray woman, just as she had Kay's capacity for understanding.

He let himself out into the rain. On the sidewalk he sheltered a match, lit a cigarette. Cars went by on the wide boulevard, a steady stream of yellow lights, singing tires. The big homes along the bluff were mostly quiet and dark. It was a very quiet neighborhood.

I shouldn't come back here any more, Sader thought. I'm getting to feel at home in a crazy kind of way. I'm beginning to get the idea you could sit in one of these piles surrounded by your stuff, and feel as miserable as if you were broke. Maybe more so. It might be frustrating to have money and to find out it really wouldn't buy just what you wanted.

He slid in behind the wheel of his car and turned the switch. A sudden unnatural tiredness ran through his body, and he felt a deep desire for sleep.

CHAPTER FOURTEEN

The ambulance was waiting but Pettis delayed it while Sader looked at Mrs. Wanderley. The turned-back canvas showed stains of old, grainy oil. In the round beam of Pettis's light the smeared features appeared hideously comic, the effect, Sader realized, of a grotesque impression of blackface. Mrs. Wanderley looked as if she had taken part in a minstrel show and had only half removed her makeup. Her clotted hair gave no hint of its blonde color, nor was there any way of telling the tint of the cloth collar stuck against her throat.

"It's her all right. She was wearing a beaver coat, though." Sader tried to concentrate on checking details. The resemblance to Kay was unmistakable, something he hadn't recognized from the snapshot, and under the circumstances, dreadful.

"We haven't found the coat," Pettis said. "Probably in there somewhere." He nodded toward the sump in the dark distance where searchlights splintered the night. "We'll get it."

"There is a taxi driver you'd better get to look at her." Sader explained their efforts to trace Mrs. Wanderley from Scotland Place, then their finding at last the cab driver who had taken her to the Veterans' Hospital. "I don't think he'd know her, though, in the shape she's in. You'll have to fix her up." Sader paused until Pettis nodded in agreement. He wanted Mrs. Wanderley to look well for Kay. "Make sure she's the woman he took out to the hospital."

"Any reason you think she isn't?"

"No. But it's important to check."

"Sure, I see that. What's his name and company?" He clicked off the light, pulled the canvas into place. Sader told him who the cab driver was while a white-coated man closed the ambulance and drove away, the lights of the big car rocking as it crossed the ruts in the road.

Pettis led the way to the office, where lights burned, the door stood open. In a chair against the counter sat Dan, smoking a cigarette. He waved wearily in greeting. Pettis said, "Now I have the two of you here, I'd like a statement of all you've done."

Dan groaned, "I'm tired. It's two o'clock in the morning. I want to go beddy-bye. Why in hell can't we at least go get some coffee?"

"I have to wait here." Pettis pulled a couple of chairs from the desks behind the counter, arranged them so that he and Sader and Dan formed a close triangle. He sat down, smiled, assumed an air of inviting confidences. Sader remembered the pose from the previous interview, but it didn't worry him as much this time. Pettis had proved fallible. His trick on Tina Griffin had backfired, frightening and angering her. She'd be a stubborn witness now.

Dan, trying to hurry the interview, began sketching his efforts to find young Ajoukian. "I guess you've interviewed his wife."

"Yes, I have," Pettis agreed.

"Well, you've got to admit that nobody in his right mind would abandon a babe like her at home to skip out for a date with Mrs. Wanderley."

"I never met Mrs. Wanderley," Pettis said, his glance cautious.

"She was forty-seven," Sader put in. "Dan imagines her as hobbling around with a cane. According to her daughter, she didn't look her age."

"She had men friends?" Pettis asked.

"No—according to all witnesses but one, she'd lost interest in men."

"You believed it?"

Sader shrugged. "I don't know. She'd been drinking heavily for quite a while. Sometimes liquor cuts down on —other things."

Pettis leaned back a little in his chair. "What was the connection then with young Ajoukian?"

Sader tried to marshal his ideas, and in the moment of silence then he caught a slight sound from outside. He thought of it at the time as a footstep and remembered Pettis's men down at the sump and glanced toward the door, expecting one of them to come in. There were other noises, spatters of rain on the tin roof, the coughing of gasoline engines on rigs in the distance, and when the sound like a footstep was not repeated he dismissed the impression that someone was out there in the dark. "Such connection as we can prove seems very trivial. It started this way. Old Mr. Ajoukian wanted to buy some oil shares from a woman who has a home here on Signal Hill, a Mrs. Margot Cole. She works as a hospital receptionist. She's getting a divorce, or at least apparently thought she might. The oil shares are probably community property. She wanted the sale kept quiet. She says she didn't want a final break with her husband. Old Mr. Ajoukian also appears shy about discussing the deal, so he might have reasons of his own for secrecy. Perhaps the presence of a partner in the deal."

"What gave you this lead?"

"The maid at Mrs. Wanderley's home overheard a telephone conversation in which the dead woman surmised that another man, a man named Charlie Ott, was back of the deal."

"Why should Mrs. Wanderley care?" Pettis wondered, sitting more erect, his expression puzzled.

"As I said, Mrs. Wanderley had become a heavy drinker. She'd also developed a dangerous temper. I think she had a previous grudge against Ott because of the failure of a real-estate deal. She was supposed to sell his duplex for him. She held a real-estate license, incidentally, though she didn't appear to need the income. Ott's place is all spruced up on the outside, as if he'd got it ready for sale. But the inside of the place is dusty, real dusty. I can't help but think that Ott had made a secret sale, gypping Mrs. Wanderley out of her commission, and then relaxed on his housekeeping. If he had still expected to display the house, he'd have kept it neat inside as well as out."

Pettis gave him a quizzical look. "Let me get this straight. Mrs. Wanderley was already mad at Ott because of a trick, selling his duplex behind her back—"

"Probably to someone she'd brought there," Sader put in.

"—and then later she decides Ott is behind Ajoukian's buying the oil shares? Still, so what? Wasn't the Cole woman getting a good price?"

"I don't know. I doubt if Mrs. Wanderley knew. Perhaps she mistook Margot Cole's desire for secrecy for something else. For embarrassment at being cheated, for instance." Sader rubbed a hand over his clipped head. "She wasn't in a logical mood that Tuesday night."

Pettis stretched his legs. "Where does young Ajoukian come in?"

"My one guess is that he took his father's place, met Mrs. Wanderley to try to calm her down."

"He gets killed for *this*?"

"They both got killed for something," Sader said evenly.

Pettis went back to Dan, questioning him about Ajoukian's stay at the bar, then entered an objection. "How could she have known he'd be there then?"

"She did a lot of drinking," Dan said. "Maybe she'd met him previously over a highball. That bar isn't as dark as some, but maybe he'd had a few and she didn't look too bad, though thinking about his wife I don't get it."

"It's too much of a coincidence," Sader protested. "I think she called the old man at home. He may have been feeling bad that day. He told her where to find his son."

Pettis looked at the two of them. "Speaking of coincidences, there's one that hits me right in the gut every time I look at you two. I guess you know what it is. How come you were called in by two such different clients, in two different towns—counties, even—about two people nobody would dream had ever met? And who then turn up in one sump hole, dead together?"

"I don't know." Sader was tense under the cop's inimical scrutiny. He began to light a new cigarette. He noticed then that Dan, who was facing the open door, was smiling as if he were seeing someone he knew. Then a sudden frown bit its way between Dan's brows.

"Come on," Pettis demanded. "Something gave you a lead. You say the Ajoukians called first, so I guess something they said gave you a lead to Mrs. Wanderley."

"We didn't contact Miss Wanderley. She came to us," Sader said. "I can't explain offhand why our agency, out of approximately a dozen, was chosen by both the Ajoukians and by Miss Wanderley." Sader had a hunch about it but didn't feel like unraveling it all to Pettis. When he and Dan had first set up the agency, they had debated the type of advertisement to be inserted in the yellow pages of the telephone book. Dan wanted something bold and aggressive, socko as he'd put it; and Sader had fought him about it. Sader had explained that the value of a private detective lay mainly in the fact that he was private. Unobtrusiveness and discretion were the things most clients wanted. The ad as finally worked out emphasized that the firm of Sader and Scarborough carried out investigations quietly and adroitly. The print was small; the wording,

Sader thought, gave off an aura of secretive shrewdness. He was thinking now to himself that secrecy and caution were the things both the Ajoukians and Kay Wanderley had been looking for. This was the logical reason both had come to them.

"People never give God credit for anything any more," Dan said. "Do you realize how long those bodies may have lain hidden if we hadn't stumbled on a connection between the two, a possible meeting up there on the Hill?"

His tone was almost idle, Sader noted; and he was still staring out into the dark through the open doorway.

Pettis outlined what he thought the chances of Divine intervention had been. He derided Sader and Scarborough as tools of heaven.

"Oh, put it on a record," Dan advised. "I'm so damned tired I can't even think straight. Why don't you let us go?"

Pettis was now cold and distant, treating them like suspicious characters he'd caught prowling an alley. "Do you think your memories might improve after some sleep?"

"I'll ask Miss Wanderley why she came to us," Sader offered.

"Ask her why she didn't report her mother missing," Pettis advised, in a voice like flint. He got to his feet.

"She *did* report her," Sader insisted, also rising.

"On your advice? And rather late, wasn't it?" Pettis's smile was thin, unforgiving. They walked out with his eyes on their backs.

The rainy night smelled cold and lonesome. Sader turned up the collar of his coat. Down at the sump a single light burned like an accusing eye. Like one of Pettis's eyes, Sader thought, mounted there to stare into their consciences. Pettis thought they were protecting their clients. It hadn't occurred to him yet that they were fresh out of customers.

The case of Perry Ajoukian was closed. The missing Mrs. Wanderley was found. Neither of them would ever be in good shape again, but they were at least accounted for. When had it been, if ever, Sader wondered, that he and Dan might have prevented the double murder?

Never, he decided.

There was no sense to these killings, excluding that of Mullens, who had died for his caution and his greed. Mullens had had information about something. He hadn't said what, but Sader remembered, getting into his car, that there were two items missing so far. The fur coat and the gun.

Maybe Mullens had known something about one of these.

Or again, he just might have known what had happened to the vine beside the office door.

Sader awoke with the sound of the shot ringing in his head.

He pushed, fought instinctively against something coiled about him, only realizing in the next moment that he was still in bed, still wrapped in the bedclothes, and that he held the telephone in his right hand. He jerked the receiver back against his ear.

While he listened his mind backtracked. Hazily he remembered the phone ringing, his taking the instrument off its cradle, then something worried and imperative— Dan's voice telling him something he'd been too deep in sleep to catch. The effort to awake. Dan's insistence, Dan's strange anger. These he could half recall, though he had no memory of what Dan had said. Then there had been the shot, a jarring unmistakable sound in the receiver. He had jerked awake at last.

He clicked on the bedside lamp and waited. At the other end of the wire he could hear muffled movement, cautious rustlings, and little bumps, as if someone were tidying up very quietly around a sleeping guest. Sader said, "Dan!" into the phone and the movement came to a halt. There was a final moment during which he heard breathing. Then the phone went dead.

Sader wasted no time in jiggling the receiver. He dialed Dan's home. After a couple of minutes Dan's aunt answered, a ladylike elderly voice full of drowsy confusion. "Is Dan at home?" Sader lifted his wrist to look at his watch. It was three-fifteen.

"Just a moment, please. I'll bring him." Sader knew the house; he heard her footsteps go down the hall, then slowly climb the stairs; and while he waited, his nerves crawled. When she came back she was still confused. "Well, he doesn't seem to have come in yet."

She was too polite to ask questions, though she must have known Sader's voice. He was in too much of a hurry for explanations. He said, "Thanks," and hung up, to lift the phone again at once and dial police headquarters. "Send somebody up to the office of Sader and Scarborough in the Warrant Building, will you? I think there may have been an accident there." Sader was out of bed now, putting on clothes with one hand while he gave the desk officer his name, occupation, the number of the office and why he thought there might have been a gun fired.

When he hung up he put on his shoes, buckled his belt, grabbed the coat off a chair, and headed out of the apartment. In about twelve minutes he slewed to the curb in front of his office. Everything was closed now. The street lights burned above deserted pavements wet with recent rain. As he ran toward the dark door of the building, a police car rounded the nearest corner. He didn't wait. He entered the narrow vestibule, ran up the stairs. A light burned behind the glass of his office door.

He tried the door, found it locked, took out his keys, cursed his hands because they trembled under nervous pressure. When he got the door open he rushed through into the inner office. Dan was there, lying on his desk, the fingers of his right hand touching the base of the phone.

Sader walked quickly to stand beside him. He forced himself to look at Dan, to examine the wound in his face. It was ugly, just below the left eye. The remarkable thing was that Dan was still alive, that the labored breathing, clogged, fluttering, still went on. Dan's flesh was warm, though his fingers felt slack and nerveless. Sader turned as the cops came in. "Will you get an ambulance? He just might have a chance." Saying it, Sader didn't believe it. There was too much blood. The bullet must be buried in Dan's brain. He'd die without ever regaining consciousness. Soon, perhaps.

One cop went down to call for an ambulance on his radio. The other one listened to Sader's explanation. Sader told him—he suspected, not too coherently—about the Ajoukian and Wanderley affairs, Mullens's murder, their conference on the Hill that night with Pettis.

"We were through," Sader concluded. "I don't know what he was doing here."

"Maybe somebody asked him to meet them here."

"It's possible. You can check with his aunt." Then Sader remembered that Dan's aunt had gone to call him from his room; she hadn't known he wasn't at home. "No, that isn't it. He never did go home. He came here." Sader took out cigarettes, offered the pack to the cop. The cop said he didn't smoke. Sader lit a cigarette for himself, walked around, feeling the tendons jerk in his shoulders, the trembling in his wrists. Old drunks always shake, he jeered at himself inwardly. And Papa, you had your share. The urge to open Dan's desk and get out Dan's bottle ran through him like a whipsaw.

He went out into the other room and had a drink from the water bottle in its stand, forcing himself to pause there afterward, to smoke slowly, to hold the cigarette rigidly steady. The cop told him not to touch anything, they'd have fingerprint men up here presently. Sader heard him through a fog of desire, the ache to relax his guard just this once, to throw liquor down himself until his nerves quit yammering.

When the ambulance came he trailed it to the hospital. He tried to go in with Dan at the emergency entrance, but the nurses sent him around to the front. He waited in the big room filled with couches and lamps while the doctors upstairs worked on Dan. When he inquired at the desk, the receptionist informed him that Dan had gone into surgery.

Sader paused in turning away. "Does a Mrs. Margot Cole work here?"

"She's off tonight," the substitute explained.

Sader rubbed the stubble of hair above his temple. Sure she was off–hadn't he met her after midnight at Milton's pig concession? He went back to the waiting room, aware that his thinking was slow and fuzzy. He wasn't picking up the pieces quickly enough. He stood in the middle of the room, looking at nothing, aware only hazily of the surprised regard of a couple who were waiting, as he was, from some word from upstairs.

Why couldn't he remember what Dan had tried to tell him on the phone? Was there a block, a will to disbelieve? All that had stayed with him was Dan's anger, words that hammered without penetrating.

He went out into the lobby, found the telephone booth, shut himself in. He called Dan's aunt, a hatred for the job like a bad taste in his mouth, and told her what had happened, how he'd come to call her earlier, where Dan was. He lied about what he thought Dan's chances were, but she knew, anyway. She begged him to make the doctors keep Dan alive until she could see him.

Sader went to the desk for more dimes, shut himself in the booth again, rang telephone numbers. Margot Cole didn't answer; neither did Milton Wanderley. Charlie Ott's line gave a busy signal. At the Ajoukians', the nurse came on, sounding waspish, and told him neither Mrs. Ajoukian nor the old man were to be disturbed. Tina Griffin wasn't listed in the book. Probably she lived in an apartment house, shared a house phone there. After a long hesitation, Sader put in a dime and dialed the Wanderley house.

He had expected Annie, but Kay came on the wire. She sounded infinitely weary, washed-out, and all he could think of was the way she'd looked when he had left her, pale and small against the pillows.

He said, "This is Sader. I had to ask you a question."

"Yes, Mr. Sader. What is it?"

"Did my partner, Dan Scarborough, call you anytime after midnight tonight?"

"Not that late, no." There was an empty moment, a pause as if she expected an explanation from Sader. "Is something the matter?"

"He was shot in our office less than an hour ago."

She caught her breath. The small sound, full of fear, brought her suddenly closer in his mind, and he imagined the tousled hair, eyes heavy with sleep, the soft swell of her breasts in the V neck of the housecoat. "I'm—I'm dreadfully sorry. I don't know what else to say, except that I'm sort of numb. Since I've known Mother is dead, nothing else seems to register. Nothing else matters at all." Another pause. "Is he badly hurt?"

Sader couldn't have said why he suddenly knew that she expected him to tell her Dan was dead. The knowledge was there, as real as if he could hold it in his hand. He tried to force it from his mind. Then he argued with himself. Considering what had happened to her, why shouldn't she take for granted that Dan's injuries had already resulted in his death?

"I don't think he has much chance," Sader answered finally.

"Let me know when there's something definite."

"Yes, I will." Sader felt sweat on his palm against the phone. "I'm sorry for what happened at your house tonight. I did what I thought was best."

"Yes, I–I appreciate that. Good night, Mr. Sader."

"Good night."

He went back to the waiting room and propped himself into the corner of a couch, drowsed off into half sleep, half nightmare. He awoke once to find Dan's aunt crying beside him; he took for granted that Dan was dying. But when he finally managed to rouse himself, after six, he learned at the desk that by some miracle Dan was still alive and might continue to live.

CHAPTER FIFTEEN

In the gray light of the rainy dawn, Sader left the café on Pine Avenue and walked to his office in the Warrant Building. He went upstairs, found the door unlocked, was still frowning over this when he stopped at the inner doorway, seeing Pettis watching him across Dan's desk.

"Come in," Pettis said. He had papers spread out on the desk. "I want you to go over this stuff with me. The Long Beach detectives say it was what your partner was working on when he was shot. It seems to be something you did."

Sader walked over to stand beside him. The spread-out sheets were the ones he had typed the evening before and concerned his visit to the field office, the encounter there with Tina Griffin and Pettis, the following interview at the Ajoukian place.

Sader went to his own desk and sat down. "Yes, I wrote that last night."

"What was in it for Scarborough?"

"I don't know." Sader made no attempt to punch through the fuzzy curtain in his brain. "When he telephoned me this morning, I was asleep. I was holding the phone when he was shot. The sound of the shot woke me. I can't remember what he was saying just before that."

Pettis wasn't pretending to be friendly, eager to believe. He looked irritable, sleep-hungry. "Okay. You've got some stuff here I didn't know about. This Mrs. Griffin, recognizing Ajoukian at the office."

"I just surmised that. You can check it by confronting old Ajoukian with the woman—when the doctor says you can do it without endangering his health."

Some grim lines settled around Pettis's mouth.

Sader began to light a cigarette. "Have you talked to Mr. Ott?"

"We did. He had some harsh things to say about you, Sader."

Sader smiled a little. "I tried to call him this morning, as soon as they got Dan to the hospital. His line seemed to be busy. I remembered that he might have left the phone off the cradle when he went out."

"You don't like him, do you? Why do you keep trying to throw suspicion on him?"

"He lied to me," Sader said. "He gave me a long spiel about how he hated old Ajoukian. I think he was covering a deal—the deal Mrs. Wanderley got wind of."

"You're saying he murdered her and young Ajoukian to keep them from spoiling his purchase of Mrs. Cole's oil shares? It's farfetched, Sader."

"They were killed because of *something*," Sader pointed out.

"Who else did you check?"

Sader unbuttoned his coat, shoved it behind him on the chair. "All of them except Tina Griffin. She isn't listed."

"Including Miss Wanderley?" Pettis asked, a tomcat note in his voice.

"She was the only one I could prove to be at home."

Pettis shuffled the papers around. "Now, this visit you paid to the Ajoukians yesterday—was this the first time you'd met the old man?"

"Yes. When we were offered the job of finding young Ajoukian, I put my partner on it."

"Why?"

"People instinctively trust Dan. He's big, assured, young, energetic. Cheerful. When the father phoned us, he sounded prostrated. As a matter of fact, young Mrs. Ajoukian told Dan later the old man had had a fainting fit, had let her pick out an agency to handle the job for him."

"The girl picked you out, hmmm?" Pettis made it sound significant.

"Neither Dan nor I had ever heard of the Ajoukians before. Oh, no—I'd read something in the papers now and then, Ajoukian being accused of selling something he'd swiped off a rig when nobody was looking. That was years ago, though. I didn't know anything about the family since, about the house in Garden Grove. The money."

Pettis's nose seemed to sharpen. "The old man's got lots of the green stuff."

"And nobody now to leave it to."

"His son's wife," Pettis reminded.

"I have the feeling they aren't fond of each other."

"You got that impression on your visit yesterday?" Pettis looked down at the typewritten sheets as if searching for information. "Where does that leave the girl? Does he mean to put her out?"

"I don't think so. I think he depends on her for a lot of things. He's a heller with his nurses, so they don't last long and the girl has to fill in while she rustles somebody new from the nurses' registry. He'd have a damned good chance of dying there all alone if she wasn't with him to smooth things."

"Okay. What brought Miss Wanderley to your office?"

"I haven't asked her yet."

"Got any ideas?"

"None."

"Sader, I expected more co-operation since your partner got it. He found something in these papers"—Pettis tapped the sheets on the desk—"that gave him a clue. He decided to talk to the person he suspected, first. He let that person, the murderer of the Wanderley woman and young Ajoukian and the office man, Mullens, get near enough to shoot him. It speaks of close acquaintance. Perhaps even liking. Doubt of the murderer's guilt."

"I figured that out," Sader said sharply.

"Now, Scarborough hadn't met a lot of these people you've been seeing. I don't think he'd met Mr. Ott. Had he talked to Mrs. Cole? To Milton Wanderley? Or to Tina Griffin?"

"He knew who they were and what I thought of each of them," Sader answered, "because we'd talked it all over. He must have hit a fresh trail. I can't think how." The desire for sleep burned behind Sader's eyes. The hours spent in the hospital waiting room had left an unendurable tiredness. "I've got to get some rest before I can think."

Pettis slapped a hand on the papers. "I'll take these along. Okay?"

"Sure." Sader looked around the room. Nothing seemed out of place. Dan's desk blotter was gone, the top of the desk wiped clean of Dan's blood. It seemed the only change here. "I guess there weren't any fingerprints."

"Plenty," Pettis grunted. "But my guess is, they'll turn out to belong to innocent people."

"What about the gun?"

Pettis was rising. "It could be the same as the one used to shoot Mrs. Wanderley, young Ajoukian, and Mullens. We'll know when we've tested the bullet they took out of your partner's head."

This was the first Sader had known of it. "They got the bullet?"

Pettis nodded. "Out of Mullens, too."

The phone rang. Sader turned over in bed and felt for the table without opening his eyes. He wanted to hang on to sleep, to inert oblivion. He took the phone off its cradle and laid it down. It made crackling sounds.

After a while he pulled it over next to his ear and still without looking listened to what it had to say. ". . . this ought to be good for some publicity. You guys like that, don't you? Where's the old commercial instinct?"

"Talk sense," Sader muttered.

"Mr. Sader?"

"Speaking."

"You want to make a statement for the press, Mr. Sader?"

"What about?"

"Haven't you heard? They've arrested your client on fraud charges."

Sader lay still, feeling the cool air of morning that filled the room. Behind the closed venetian blinds the sun was shining, all the clouds had drifted on, and a mockingbird who had neglected so far to fly south was trying a few trills and obbligatos from a perch on a telephone pole. The sense of rightness about all this clashed with the voice on the phone.

"Play that back again, will you?"

"We'd like to know what you think about your client, Mrs. Ajoukian, being charged with fraud. She's getting out on bail. But the smear remains."

"Who had her arrested?"

"Her father-in-law."

"Please quote me as saying—" Sader tried to think of what he ought to say. Something meaningless, optimistic, polite. All at once he slammed the phone back into its cradle and sat up. There was a time for work and a time for sleep. Right now the people involved in this affair were busy doing things to each other. He hurried with a shower, dressed in clean clothes, went out to his car. He made better time to Garden Grove than he ever had before.

Nobody answered the doorbell. He walked around to the rear of the house, into a yard studded with lemon trees, shut in by walls of ivy, and found the rear entry unlocked. The kitchen did justice to the rest of the place. It was divided into two parts. Half was brick and redwood, with picnic-style furnishings. Probably the architect had called it a barbecue. The other section was glass, tile, and steel, as antiseptic as a hospital. On the big white range, a frying pan full of bacon was frizzling into ash. Sader stopped to turn off the burner.

A maple breakfast table was set for one. An electric coffee maker gave forth an odor which reminded Sader how many hours had passed since he'd eaten breakfast in the café on Pine Avenue.

He went through the breakfast room to an inner hall. About ten feet ahead of him, old Mr. Ajoukian lay spread out on his back, the white blanket under him. He wore a pair of cerise flannel pajamas, a brown toweling bathrobe. Sader hurried to kneel beside him. The fierce old eyes came open in a bitter stare.

"Mr. Ajoukian—"

Mr. Ajoukian bared his teeth. They were yellow and uneven. The lips had no color in them. The skin around the mouth was as tough, as wrinkled, as elephant hide. "Go away, faker." The breath came out on a wheeze, almost obliterating the sound of the words.

"Let me guess," Sader said, looking down at him. "You ripped into your nurse, and she quit. You had your son's wife arrested. Then you decided to cook breakfast for yourself to show everybody how independent you could be."

"Get out!"

"Do you want me to help you back to bed?"

"Go to hell!" The old man turned over on his belly and hunched up his knees and tried to crawl. Sader squatted, neither helping nor hindering. When the old man fell on his face and cursed slobbering curses, Sader still waited, moving only to light a cigarette. "Well—give me a hand!"

Sader rose and stepped back. "I think I'd better call your doctor."

"I don't want a doctor!" Old Mr. Ajoukian yowled like a cat. "I want some peace and quiet around here, no women clattering, no talk, questions!"

Sader bent down, jerked him to his feet. The rough handling surprised the old man and he bent on Sader a look of speculative hatred. Sader stooped, got the blanket, tossed it around the elder Ajoukian's shoulders. "Can't you walk?"

"Sure I can walk." Ajoukian tried to assume a baron's strut, probably his usual mode of locomotion, but on the third step he went to his knees.

Sader waited. Still on his knees, Ajoukian got over against the wall and inched upward. He patted the tinted plaster. "I built all this. Nice house. Good stuff in it."

"No handles on the walls. It's what you need." Sader turned as if to go.

"Wait!" Erect now, old Ajoukian seemed suddenly stronger, as if some infusion of bitterness had stiffened his back. "I got a few things to say. That girl, that thief— I want you to see she stays in jail. Take me out to the table. I got breakfast cooking. I'll give you something to eat . . . drink. We'll plan it." An almost jovial brightness illumined the monkey-like face. Old Ajoukian's hands shook with excitement.

"I'll help you to the table." Sader offered an arm; the weight that came on it was surprisingly light, unsteady. He felt as if a rooster had perched there, digging in claws. "You'll have to set a few things straight, though. Like your being in Mullens's office the night before he died."

Old Ajoukian waved a hand. "It was nothing. No matter, now. He'd found Perry's car. That's all there was."

Sader kept his eyes on the maple table the other side of the open door. "Where did he find the car?"

"In a garage. A vacant place, for sale. Couple of blocks from the office. He had me come late at night. He showed me the car." Suddenly the old man threw his head back with a cackle of laughter. "I was scared for a while, thinking maybe Perry was in bad trouble, hiding, needing help. Now I don't think so. Perry can take care of himself. He's my boy, the rascal!"

The shock of it ran through Sader like ice water. The old man didn't know his son was dead. Then another idea crossed Sader's mind; he glanced uneasily at the cackling old man. Was his mind broken by grief? Was he crazy?

The bright, brimming eyes met Sader's knowingly, confidently. There was no indication that a full quota of intelligence wasn't operating behind the wrinkled mask. Sader said, "How much did Mullens want—and for what?"

"He wanted a few thousands of dollars," Ajoukian tittered. "He kept telling me his mother needed an operation."

"Who was his silence supposed to protect? Your son?"

Ajoukian nodded. "He said Perry might be in trouble."

Through Sader's memory straggled something from his interview with Mullens. Mullens had speculated, rather significantly, whether Mrs. Wanderley might be hiding out from a drunk-driving charge. Sader, inching the tottering old man through the door to the breakfast room, tried to pry a meaning from Mullens's remark in the light of what Ajoukian had just said.

Mullens must have seen young Ajoukian's car, followed it to the vacant garage where it had been hidden. Had there been an accident on the way, some hint that the driver wasn't adequate? It was the only thing Sader could think of.

Sader pulled out a chair beside the maple table. "Sit down, Mr. Ajoukian. I'll fix you some more bacon in a minute. You wouldn't want that burned stuff. But first tell me—whom have you seen this morning? You must have talked to somebody. You managed to have your daughter-in-law arrested."

Old Ajoukian's bright mood seemed to falter. He plucked uneasily at the collar of his robe. "I called an attorney out from Santa Ana, showed him the evidence."

"And what was the evidence?"

"A forged power of attorney she claims was signed by Perry before he disappeared."

"You questioned her about it?"

"No. The lawyer did. The doctor was here. He wouldn't let us talk for long. I told the lawyer the paper was a fake, she was stripping my bank accounts, buying foolishness. Soon there wouldn't be anything left."

"This attorney was somebody you'd had dealings with before?"

A crafty look flickered in the old man's face. "No. He's a young fellow. Smart. On his toes."

Sader smelled trickery. The old man had called in a young, perhaps inexperienced attorney who had had no background in his affairs. "I'm surprised he didn't advise you to go slow in such an affair involving a member of your family. How much had she stolen?"

Ajoukian waved a hand vaguely. "He knows."

"Are the withdrawals recent? Since your son's disappearance?"

"Does it matter?"

"Someone should have told you, Mr. Ajoukian. Your son is dead. He's been dead all these days since you last saw him."

The clawlike hands convulsed on the table. The rapacious mouth turned slack. "What . . . what do you say?" He waited while Sader told him again. "I don't believe it." But there were indications of belief, nevertheless; a kind of inward searching, of totting up old clues, old fears.

"You shouldn't have had his widow put in jail," Sader went on. He hated this old man who stank of greed, of corrupting avarice; he hated him so much there was only obliquely any trace of pity. "It's going to get you a horrible name in the newspapers. Are you going to claim, now, that she was stealing from your dead son's estate?"

Old man Ajoukian wagged his head. "I don't know."

"Didn't your son own anything? If he did, it's hers now."

The old man struggled with words, then spat them fiercely. "A half of all I have. His. I gave it when they married."

"Well, you'd better call the attorney and explain the set-up. She can't be robbing you if it's already hers."

The old man put his hands on the table, on either side of the plate. His jaw shook, and he drooled. "Never! I'll never take back the charges."

"How much did you give Mullens?"

"Not a cent!"

"Where is your son's car?"

Old Ajoukian wagged his head from side to side.

Sader bent close to him. "Mrs. Wanderley called the house Tuesday night. You answered. She accused you of cheating Mrs. Cole on her oil shares, of being partners in the deal with Charlie Ott."

Ajoukian's clawlike hands moved restlessly on the table.

"Mrs. Wanderley was raising so much hell, you decided your son had better see her. You told her she could reach him at the bar in the Chuck-A-Luck. That was a mistake, Mr. Ajoukian."

There was a wheezing noise from between the old man's teeth.

"That phone call took him to his death." Sader waited, letting the words sink in. The old man sat very still, hunched over, the wrinkled face bent toward the table. "Mrs. Wanderley was very drunk. She was violent. Didn't you have any hint of danger to your son?"

Ajoukian's tongue stole out to wet his lips. "I thought you were going to fix my breakfast!"

"If I stay, I'll break your neck. Anyway, your daughter-in-law will be home pretty soon, Mr. Ajoukian, and I think you'd better get what service you can from her while she's still with you. Let her cook breakfast. She's not going to be with you very long. Not if she has good sense."

CHAPTER SIXTEEN

Sader jerked the wheel, sent the car spinning into the graveled space beside the Chuck-A-Luck Barbecue. A side entry led to the bar; it was locked. Sader went into the main dining room. It was big, ranchy in style and there were about a half dozen people eating breakfast there. Most of them looked as if they'd been up all night. A waitress minced over to Sader and said, "Yes, sir?"

"I'd like to use the phone."

She jerked her head toward the inner entry to the bar. "In there. Rear corner."

The bar was dark. Sader found the phone fixed to the wall, no booth here as Dan had said. He dialed the hospital, got Dan's floor supervisor. The nurse informed him Dan was doing as well as could be expected. "Aren't they all?" Sader ground out. "I want to know if he's conscious."

"No, sir, he has not regained consciousness," said the supervisor stiffly.

"Will he live?"

There was a flinty silence, and then the nurse said, "I

could not make a prognosis, sir. Perhaps you could call Dr. Heffelmaier."

"Good God," Sader said, slammed down the receiver. Silly to make the woman mad; he'd have to talk to her again. There was a lot he wanted to know. He'd have to keep the rage down, though it was hard to do when he thought of Dan. He walked out to the dining room, met the waitress again. "Is the bartender around anywhere?"

"No, sir. He's not here yet."

Sader gave her his card and a dollar. "Ask him to call me at the office around noon."

"Yes, sir. Thank you, sir. Will you be having breakfast?"

"Could you put some coffee in a carton? I'll take it with me."

"Yes, sir. Will a two-cup carton be okay?"

"Fine."

He talked with the waitress mechanically, his real thoughts busy with the Ajoukians, with Charlie Ott, the Cole woman. When he reached Long Beach he turned north on Cherry, crested the Hill, stopped finally at 3132 Redwood. It looked the same as it had. Someone had watered the begonias and the ferns along the porch, so that water stood in puddles on the cement. Mama duck led her family eternally into the shelter of the willow tree. Sader rang the bell and after a couple of minutes Margot Cole looked out at him.

Sader plunged into it. "I know you're sore. You can call me anything you like. I just—"

She surprised him. "Come in, Mr. Sader. I'm not mad any more."

He followed her into the neat warm house. The black hair coiled on her neck was freshly combed, her makeup showed no disarray, her green cotton housecoat seemed just out of the laundry. But all this spruceness, Sader felt, was a front for tiredness and grief. She seemed bowed by some inner weight. Despair, perhaps. He waited uncomfortably while she examined him with her strange blue eyes.

"I've done a lot of thinking." She motioned him into a chair, sat down facing him. "It was silly to blame you because my husband left me again. He just wanted an excuse, anything to flare up over. If it hadn't been your visit, and the business with Ajoukian coming out, he'd have found something else." She twisted her hands in her lap. "I've had the radio on, heard the news. I learned about your partner being shot. And about Felicia's coat."

"Wait a minute—"

"She wasn't involved in any affair with that young man. They were murdered. I—I can't quite see how the murder might have happened because the Ajoukians were buying my oil shares. But I'll tell you all about it, anyway."

"The coat—"

Her blue eyes sharpened. "Hadn't you heard? They've drained that sump. Felicia's coat, the beaver coat, was in the bottom of it, tied up around a big stone."

Sader felt something cold slide across the skin. "Weighted," he said.

"Yes. It must have been done after she was dead, mustn't it?"

"I guess so." Sader wondered if Kay knew by now, if

they'd had her up to look at the coat, if she'd seen the slime and smelled the stench and so knew at last the kind of place her mother had lain all those days and nights. "I've been out of touch with what's going on at the sump. Since my partner was shot."

She leaned toward him dry-eyed, though there was somehow about her an aura of tears. "He was the fourth, wasn't he? First there was Mullens, the man in the office—"

"No. First there was your friend, Mrs. Wanderley," Sader said heavily. "She got mad, perhaps drunkenly and unreasonably—but mad, anyhow—because Ajoukian was buying those oil shares. She seemed to think Charlie Ott had a finger in the deal."

Margot Cole's expression changed gradually to one of astounded anger. "What?"

"The maid, Annie, overheard Mrs. Wanderley in a conversation with young Ajoukian. Tuesday night, just before she left her house on Scotland Place. Mrs. Wanderley was saying, among other things, that Charlie Ott was at the bottom of the deal somewhere."

"How could he be?" Mrs. Cole said, the anger growing uncertain. "He hasn't any cash. All he owns is that duplex. He hadn't sold it yet."

"I think he had," Sader told her. "And I see now his reason for being secretive. He had Ajoukian front for him because he'd closed the deal on the duplex behind Mrs. Wanderley's back, cheating her out of her commission." The rage began to flow through Sader again, a tide he couldn't control. He trembled, thinking of the cheap lies, the slimy double dealing, that had confused the case.

Sader got up, strode back and forth, smoking furiously. Mrs. Cole watched him as if in surprise. "If Felicia was cheated that way, she wouldn't have liked it. It wouldn't have been the money. The letter of the law was very important to her."

Sader agreed with her. Mrs. Wanderley had come from a family whose wealth had been built up through the manipulation of mortgages, of property. A trick like Ott's was an outrage to her code. He said, "I'm going down to talk to Ott, to get the truth from him."

"Do you want me to go along?"

"Yes, if you want to."

She hurried into a coat, put on the hat with the brim he remembered from last night. It didn't take long to go over to Cherry Avenue, to top the Hill and turn on Ott's street at its base. All the time he drove, scraps burned their way through Sader's mind. Mostly he thought about Dan, about Dan's head fallen on the desk in a puddle of bright red blood. As they stopped in front of Ott's two-story establishment, she said, "He's fixed it up."

"A paint job." Sader opened the car door for her. They went up the steps to the front door together. All at once Sader put a hand on her arm. "Wait here, will you? I'll take a look around back." He stepped off the porch, followed a cement walk to the rear yard. The lawn needed mowing, the borders were straggly, and some poinsettias against the rear fence had sagged under the rain and hadn't been retied. He saw the traces of neglect, remembered the dust inside the house. It all fitted the pattern. Ott had sold secretly, and somehow just before her death Mrs. Wanderley had caught on. Sader went up three steps to the back porch and rang a bell. Then he put his hand on the door handle, turned it, went in.

Charlie Ott was at the sink, under a wide window, opening a bottle of whiskey. He turned as Sader came in. "What—" The blankness fled from his eyes as they pinpointed with anger. "What the devil do you think you're doing?"

Sader walked over to the sink and grabbed the front of Ott's shirt. The fabric felt greasy, worn, and the man himself gave off an unwashed odor. He'd been drinking heavily, Sader thought. But not too heavily to forget what he had in a drawer under the drain-board. Out of the corner of his eye Sader saw Ott's fingers closing around a cleaver.

He hit Ott a chopping blow with the side of his hand against the windpipe. At the same moment, as he tried to duck, the blunt edge of the cleaver came down on Sader's shoulder. He moved back. Ott strangled, sucking breath, clawing at his throat with his free hand. Sader's shoulder burned for an instant, then grew numb.

He tried to flex his left hand but the fingers moved slowly, nervelessly. With his right, he knocked the cleaver from Ott's fingers, dragged the man by the front of his shirt into the front room, pushed him into a chair. Ott staggered, clutching his windpipe. He made bubbling noises from the chair. Sader went to the front door, opened it, led Mrs. Cole back into the living room. She looked at Ott, at Ott's convulsed features, as if she'd never noticed them before. "What's the matter with him?"

"He's getting his breath," Sader told her. He went to a sofa, sat down on its arm, tried to get his cigarettes out with the numb fingers of his left hand. It didn't work. The whole arm tingled now with an electric warmth. "When he can talk, I'll ask him about Mrs. Wanderley."

The strange blue eyes circled the room; her heavy face grew disapproving. "It's awfully dusty in here."

"He'd sold the place. It must be in escrow. He didn't have to keep it neat any more."

She regarded Sader with curiosity. "Is that what gave you the idea he'd cheated Felicia?"

"Partly." Sader had been keeping track of Ott. He noted that the other man was getting control of himself, that a cunning light had begun to burn behind the prolonged distress. Sader stood up, walked over to Ott, put a foot on the rung of the maple arm chair. "Mr. Ott, I want information. I want to know when and why you contacted Ajoukian. I want to know when you sold your place and to whom. Mostly, I want to know when Mrs. Wanderley found out you'd gypped her on her commission."

Ott lay flaccid, staring; but Sader was suspicious of the continuing reaction. Ott's neck was fat, the blow hadn't been as heavy as Sader might have made it. All at once he seemed to make whistling attempts to speak. Temporarily off guard, Sader bent closer to listen.

Ott's big fat hands came up and clamped on Sader's throat, the thumbs digging in, cutting off breath. Sader's army training had left him some automatic reactions; and this was one. His hands clenched together, rose in a sharp jerk that spread Ott's arms, broke his hold. Then

Ott, quickly for a man in his shape, lifted a knee, trying for Sader's groin. Sader stepped briefly aside, stayed there until Ott had sprung to his feet. Then he buried his right hand to the wrist in Ott's belly.

Ott folded over, clutched his midriff, grunted, went to his knees. Mrs. Cole had retreated nervously to the door to the hall.

Sader went back to the arm of the couch, forced himself to sit down there and to wait until Ott was through retching and wheezing and had regained the chair. Then he said reasonably, "All right. Start talking."

"I'll have your license for this," Ott got out. "Yes, sir. You won't be no private dick no more. Not if I can help it."

"I'm not a damned bit interested," Sader told him. "What I care about now is the attempt to kill Dan Scarborough, my partner. I resent having my business associates picked off like owls on a fence." He got up and started for Ott again, but now the big man put up a placating hand.

"Hold your horses. I didn't shoot anybody. Your partner, nor Felicia, nor young Ajoukian. Nor Mullens, the guy in the office. You've got a screw loose, coming here to pick on me."

Sader stopped a few feet from Ott and they regarded each other for a couple of minutes in silence. Ott must not have liked what he saw, for he began in a whining tone, "It wasn't my fault, selling the place behind Felicia's back. She brought an old coot up here, a regular skinflint, one of those retired corn merchants, seventy if he was a day, and a little bit later in the week he was back saying he liked the place but couldn't meet the price. And couldn't I shave it a little. Like, for instance, by the amount of the agent's commission."

Sader asked, "What was Mrs. Wanderley asking for the place?"

"Thirty-five."

"Thirty-five thousand?" Sader looked at Mrs. Cole to see if she believed this. She was staring at Ott in indignation.

Ott hurried on. "It's not just the house and lot. All these places along here are being whipstocked by those rigs to the north of us. We got oil rights. Hell, they're worth at least forty a month."

"Okay, you made the sale. It's in escrow now?"

"Yeah," Ott said sullenly.

"You haven't got the money yet, then."

Under the fuzzy gray hair, Ott's face took on some color. "That's how I went to Ajoukian. I heard Margot say she was going to raise money on her oil shares. What I've owned here, in connection with my place, gave me the idea to invest in some more. I couldn't come right out and offer to buy."

"I wouldn't have sold them to you," Margot Cole said.

"Yeah, I know. Afraid your old man would find out." Ott regarded the woman with open dislike. "I'll bet when he left he didn't even say, kiss my foot. He sure made a sap out of you."

She quivered a little as if a chill had swept through her. "Keep your mouth shut about my affairs, Charlie."

Ott seemed to gain confidence from having scored as he had with Mrs. Cole. "I called old Ajoukian, went out to his place later, and we cooked it all up. He was going to advance the cash for a share in the oil deal. Margot wasn't to know. He figured he'd get a better price than I could. Knowing the old buzzard, I guess he could at that." Ott was sitting straighter in the chair. "You get one thing through your thick head right now, Sader. I wouldn't kill no dame over a thirty-five-thousand-dollar deal. That's chicken feed these days."

Sader turned his back, walked over to the windows. The sun showed the Hill against the sky to the north, the pincushion forest of oil derricks, a silver tank or two. He thought abstractly of all the millions of dollars in wealth that had come out of the brown heights, pipes that reached down to finger the depths, the people who lived in cities at other ends of the earth on this money and had never so much as smelled the dry pungent odor of oil. He thought too about Mrs. Wanderley. "It's possible Mrs. Wanderley's murder wasn't premeditated, that it was the desperate impulse of a moment. She went out raging drunk. Someone may have protected himself."

"You can't prove she was raging at me," Ott said cunningly. "I didn't meet her that Tuesday night." The smugness jarred.

Sader said slowly, "She was picked up by a cab about five o'clock on Wednesday morning. Just a few blocks from here."

"I'm telling you, I didn't see her." But Ott's pale eyes were nervous. He supported his paunch in his laced hands, leaned forward as if to impress Sader with his sincerity. "She didn't come here."

Sader turned back to the window. He sensed that a glance passed between Mrs. Cole and the fat man. She cleared her throat and said unevenly, "I'd like to explain, Mr. Sader, that Felicia didn't learn of the oil deal from me. Nor, I doubt, from Mr. Ajoukian."

"I think she put together scraps of conversation she heard at your party," Sader said. The point had little importance, he thought. Mrs. Wanderley, already suspicious of Ott's trickery, had been quick to spot the evidence Ott wanted kept concealed. His mind returned to the detail of the trip on Wednesday morning. It didn't fit in with any other part of the evidence. Strike out what the cab driver had said, and he'd figure it this way: Felicia Wanderley had left home at eleven o'clock Tuesday night, had walked several blocks looking for a cab or a bus, had finally gotten a ride on one of the other lines that crossed town just above Ocean Avenue. Broadway and Third both had buses on them. Probably the maneuver had been born of raging impatience rather than a desire to throw off anyone trying to trace her. She'd transferred downtown to the Cherry Avenue line, left the bus near the military academy on the Hill, walked east to Mullens's office.

There she had met young Ajoukian and the two of them had been murdered, their bodies thrown into the oil sump.

This had no sense in it, he admitted to himself; but the line of action was at least clean, straight, without a postscript like the cab trip, which had the meaninglessness of nightmare.

Throw out the cab trip, and what have you? he thought. Well, you had an impostor there in Mrs. Wanderley's coat and scarf, for one thing. He remembered in that moment the cab driver's saying that the woman he'd taken to the Veterans' Hospital had carried no handbag.

He turned to look at Mrs. Cole, and her strange blue eyes met his own so intently—could it possibly be no more than imagination?—that he had the feeling her thoughts had followed his, that she had read his mind.

Ott was behind Sader, had moved silently from the chair on the balls of his feet; and in the instant of looking at Mrs. Cole, Sader caught other movement, Ott's suddenly reaching arms.

Ott pinned him from behind, then ran like a bull to crash into the wall. Sader turned his head, arched back, but the jarring collision tore breath from his lungs, sent pain flashing through his already injured shoulder. Still he managed to twist far enough to get his right elbow under Ott's double chin. He prized back Ott's head as the fat man weaved and faltered. Mrs. Cole made whimpering noises and ran out through the front door.

In spite of Sader's agonizing pressure on his throat, Ott got him into the hall. They fought, scuffling up the runner and knocking down a little table that held a vase with some dead sweet peas and ivy. At last they were at the door, which Mrs. Cole had left open. Ott fell through to the porch, gripped Sader's knees, threw him forward so that he slid down the steps to the lawn.

With surprising agility Ott ran back into the house and slammed the door.

Sader stood up, brushed mechanically at his clothes. His shoulder had pins in it, dancing along his nerves; and his arm felt dead. Worse than the pain was the sense of self-disgust, of failure, stupidity. Ott had bested him, giving him nothing he hadn't already surmised.

CHAPTER SEVENTEEN

Sader escorted Mrs. Cole to her door. Her attitude was nervous now, as if he were in danger of exploding with unpredictable violence. "I hope your partner pulls through." She offered him her hand.

Peacemaking, Sader thought. But why? "Are you going through with the deal to sell your oil shares to Ajoukian?"

"I gave him an option," she admitted. "Five hundred dollars. If he wants them, I'll have to sell." She unlocked her door, paused there. "I'll admit to you why I needed cash in a hurry. It really wasn't for a divorce. My daughter's eighteen and she wants a car. The other girls have them."

She was a woman, Sader decided, who would break her neck to keep her kids up there with the Joneses.

"Her father wouldn't have approved," Mrs. Cole added. "That doesn't matter now."

"I've been curious about your place here, in among the derricks," he said. "There are so few like it, and those not kept up like this."

"We've owned it for a long time. My children have wanted me to move during these last few years, to get a better location. But I like it here. You wouldn't think so, but it's private. There's no one watching you over the back fence. Nosy neighbors, I mean."

Well, she had a right to her preference. Sader nodded, started away. Then he looked back at her. "I guess there's nothing you can add about Mrs. Wanderley's last visit—"

"At the party? No, I've told you all I know."

Her eyes were like a couple of blue lights. She stood there watching while he got into his car and drove away.

When he pulled to a stop again, it was in front of the drilling office where Mullens had died. The door was open. A couple of men were behind the counter, along with a tall woman who wore glasses. The three of them seemed to be working over Mullens's books. Sader introduced himself. "I'd like to have Mullens's home address. I want to talk to his mother."

The elder of the two men frowned. "She's upset about her son's death."

"I won't be long. I'll be as tactful as possible," Sader promised.

After a few more minutes of argument, they divulged the address, less than a dozen blocks southeast, where homes encroached on the flank of the Hill. Sader found the place without difficulty. Right away he noted the evidence of Mullens's passion for gardening. The yard was meticulously kept, with borders of calendulas just coming into bloom, and dusty miller in twin rows beside the walk to the front porch. Sader rang the bell and waited.

It wasn't a big house; it was what you'd expect of a bookkeeper with an ailing mother to support. What was noticeable was the old-maid tidiness of the place. The woman who came to the door and looked out at Sader had the same air; she was as scrubbed, tidy, and plain as the house. She wore her thin white hair pulled back behind her ears, rolled there in a neat bun. Inside the blue gingham apron, the plain gray dress, her figure was spare and erect. "Yes, sir?"

Her voice was pleasant, but there were tears under it; and Sader, having heard the tone before, knew how little it would take to break up the interview. "My name is Sader, Mrs. Mullens. I'm a private detective. I'd like to talk to you for a little while. About your son's death."

She gasped. Her hands fluttered at the neck of the gray dress. "I'd rather . . . really, I'd rather not—"

"His wasn't the only murder in this affair, though I don't expect you to be excited about those other people," Sader said, to distract her. "It's just that I—frankly, I'm in a hole. I can't see any way out of it."

She got her eyes fixed on him again. "Are you the man whose partner was shot this morning in an office downtown?"

"Yes. My partner, Dan Scarborough, is the man who got it."

"Well . . ." Plainly, she hated letting him in to ask questions. She'd covered her grief decently, though putting it away had racked her; and she didn't want to be broken down again.

"I won't stay long," Sader said.

"Come in, then."

The parlor was old-fashioned, orderly, though full of a lot of knickknacks that Sader guessed had been gathered over a long period of years. Mrs. Mullens offered him a plush-covered chair whose mahogany armrests were carved into lions' heads. He sat down, loosened his coat, crushed down the weariness that threatened to creep through him. "I'd like to know how much your son told you about the events of last Tuesday night."

She folded her hands on her lap, pursed her lips thoughtfully. "What he was interested in was a car, Mr. Sader."

Sader waited, seeing that she wanted to compose her ideas so that she could speak briefly and be rid of him.

"He came home at about ten o'clock Tuesday night. He was very tired. He had a late snack—he'd been home earlier, you see, for dinner—and then about ten forty-five he came out of his room and said he had to go back to the office."

"He'd been working in his room?"

"I suppose so. He did have overtime hours near the end of the month. I was watching television when he left. I didn't hear him come in. The next morning, at breakfast, he said a most peculiar thing."

Sader crossed his knees, tried to relax, to concentrate upon what she was saying. He could imagine Mullens, looking at his mother across the breakfast table, across the good hearty food she had laid out for him.

"He asked my opinion, Mr. Sader. He asked if I would think it very wrong if he tried to raise cash from something he'd learned—something detrimental to a person who had a great deal of money."

Sader thought, the two with money in this affair were Mrs. Wanderley and old Ajoukian. No one else he'd met in the case could be considered wealthy. No, wait—

She was speaking again. "I told him that such a proposition could only be considered as blackmail, that my need for expensive medical treatments didn't change moral values."

"I see. What did he decide?"

"He didn't say. He was absentminded Wednesday evening. Thursday and Friday he seemed to have something—some difficulty—on his mind. I didn't ask about it. I'd raised him to be a good honest person; I couldn't admit, even to myself, that he would stray from the principles I'd taught him."

She turned her head, smoothed a doily on a table by her chair. The moment when Sader thought she must dissolve into tears dragged by; she looked at him again. "Friday night he was out very late. On Saturday morning he said he had work to do, a few hours to clear up some accounts. Before he went to the office he told me that there was a car hidden near here, in the garage of a house that is empty, for sale."

"Did he give you the address?"

"Yes, he did, Mr. Sader, and I have told it to the police. But they have forbidden me to give the address to anyone else."

A cold prickling stirred along Sader's nerves. "That means they have a stakeout on the car. The police are waiting for someone to come for it."

"The—the murderer?"

Sader nodded. "It's a pretty good hunch, but I don't think the murderer in this case will fall for it."

She inched forward on her chair. "Whose car is it?"

"It belonged to one of the victims in the sump, the young man named Perry Ajoukian. The murderer obviously drove it away from the sump during the time your son was in the office Tuesday night. I think the murderer was hoping those bodies wouldn't be found for quite a while, perhaps never."

"But they're getting rid of the old sumps on the Hill."

"Maybe the murderer didn't know about the cleanup campaign." Sader moved a bit in the stiff old-fashioned chair, trying to favor the shoulder, which still throbbed from Ott's blow. "I don't think your son knew about those dead people, Mrs. Mullens. I don't believe he deliberately withheld evidence of murder. He must have followed young Ajoukian's car, seen it hidden in the vacated property, decided that something underhanded was going on."

She nodded eagerly. "That could have been it."

"He approached Ajoukian, Sr. They met and talked Friday night in the office. Did you know that?"

"No."

"The father apparently didn't think that the evidence —the car being where it was and whatever Mullens told him about its journey there—was worth what your son expected."

Her pale old eyes flickered, brimmed with tears. "If my son did what you imply, if he tried to blackmail this man, he did it because of his loyalty to me. He did it because I need medical help, expensive help, so badly." She rose, stood stiffly, and Sader knew that their talk was over.

He thanked her at the door. "I wish you might have known more," he added. "You can never tell just what might trip them up."

"I wish I knew who killed my son," she said firmly. "Good-bye, Mr. Sader and good luck."

He went back to the car. He drove for almost thirty minutes before he was sure of the vacant house. He'd driven past twice, fast, noting the fuzzy lawn, advertising handbills on the porch, the real-estate sign on an iron peg near the steps. The house was about four blocks from Mullens's home, almost in a direct line to the office. Somebody had acted quickly after the murder. Quickly and shrewdly. When a place was vacant, up for sale, nobody looked for a car in the garage.

He parked in the block to the east and sized things up. He spotted the cops at once. One of them was trimming a hedge in a yard across the street from the vacant house. The new overalls gave it away; Pettis should be more careful, Sader thought dryly. The other cop was peddling an ice-cream cart. He went around and around the block. Business was terrible and if he'd been a real ice-cream man he'd have left in a hurry.

Sader started the car and drove slowly, looking at house numbers as if he might be a tourist. The cop trimming the hedge gave him a hard look. Sader waved to him cheerfully. On the sign by the steps he read, FOR SALE. *Reasonable. Low down payment. Call agent.* Then he saw the telephone number painted at the bottom of the sign and his foot hit the brake so hard he was almost cut in two by the wheel.

The motor conked out. The cop trimming the hedge waddled out into the street and stared in at him. "Something wrong, bud?"

"I'm looking for a place to rent," Sader said feebly.

The cop motioned with his hedge clippers. "You wanna see that place over there?"

"It's for sale," Sader pointed out. "I said, rent."

"They might rent it." The cop waited, eager for Sader to show some interest in the watched house. Sader decided he was bored clipping the hedge and wanted other work for a change. Like twisting somebody's arm to make him talk.

"Well, I could take down the telephone number." Sader, with elaborate ceremony, took out one of his cards, turned it over, and wrote down the Wanderley telephone number, under the cop's stare. "I don't much care for the yard though. Looks neglected."

"Just needs mowing." The cop stepped back. He was hot inside the stiff new overalls, Sader thought, and disappointed now too because Sader hadn't expressed a wish to prowl around the vacant house. "It's all okay otherwise."

"I might be back, after I've telephoned the agent."

Sader drove away. Grim thoughts boiled in his head. You could have coincidences all in a row, he told himself, and be surprised over them—but all at once there was one too many. As he had told Mrs. Mullens such a short while before, you never knew when you were going to trip them up.

There was a brisk sea wind stirring the trees along Scotland Place. The blue horizon at the end of the street was full of sparkle. It was a wonderful day for a walk on the beach, Sader thought, or a drive. Especially a drive. He left the car at the curb and walked to the Wanderley door and rang. When Annie came, all starched and full of manners, he said, "I've got to see her."

Annie took him inside without a word.

Kay was arranging a bowl of flowers on a cabinet in the living room. She turned as Sader came in. She was pale, he noticed; but she was wearing the rhinestones. They glittered cheerfully in the light from the terrace windows.

"Hello, Mr. Sader." She put down the tawny chrysanthemums, smoothed the waist of the dress she wore, soft green silk that fell in pleated folds. She looked awfully young in that instant. About fifteen, Sader thought.

He went close to her. The thought of the dead woman in the sump, of young Ajoukian as he'd seen him soaked in oil, Mullens on the floor of his office—these were dim now, far away. And his anger over Dan ran out like water from a sieve. You had to forgive someone as young, as beautiful, as this. "Get your hat and coat. You're coming with me."

For a moment she looked at him as if trying to read something in his face. Then she went quickly from the room. When she came back she wore the little fur jacket, the velvet hat. "Where are we going?"

"A ride."

They were almost in Santa Ana before she began to be worried. "Are you sure it's all this way from town?"

"What?" Sader turned at an intersection, headed northeast on a through boulevard, his mind on the miles ahead.

"The thing–whatever it is–you want me to see."

He shot a look sidewise. "There's nothing for you to see."

"Then–why come out here?"

"Don't you know?"

Her gloved hands tightened on her little purse. The soft mouth grew tense. "No, I can't imagine what you're talking about."

"They found the car," he said gently. "Ajoukian's car, hidden the night of the murders. Don't you see what that means? Your mother had the place listed. She'd be one of the few people who'd know right away where to go."

"I guess I just don't understand. Are you still accusing Mother of some part in the crime?"

Was this a game? "No, not any more."

"Then–what is it?"

"You knew the places she was trying to sell, didn't you?"

"Most of them."

"Figure it out, then."

Several miles slipped past under the tires. They entered a long road overhung with giant pepper trees, this side of San Bernardino. The afternoon sun threw leafy patterns and the car fled through them, as if through ghostly interlacing fingers. Finally she asked, "Is there some sort of danger?"

"You should know," he said dryly.

He sensed the unwilling fear that shook her. "Because of–of what happened to Dan?"

"I don't want to think about him."

She touched his arm. "How do you know? How can you be sure?"

"About you? Well, the idea had flickered through my mind more than once. That business with the dog had a funny ring to it. And then the delay about hiring anyone to look for her. Who told you to come to us, anyway?"

"Annie. She looked in the telephone book at the listings of private detectives. She thought the whole plan was disgusting, but since I was determined to have somebody—well, she had the idea your names, Sader and Scarborough, sounded like gentlemen."

"What a shock she must have got," Sader muttered.

She touched his arm again. "Do you know who it is?"

The leafy patterns flickered on the windshield. "Who *what* is?"

"That—that I'm in danger from."

"Pettis."

"But he's a policeman!"

Sader glanced sidewise at her. She was so fresh, so achingly beautiful, it was all he could do to keep his hands on the wheel. Under his love and his desire for her burned other things—self-hatred, mostly—but these he crushed down. "Didn't Pettis ask questions about that vacant house on the Hill?"

"The one Mother had listed to sell? Yes, he did. He asked for her account book, too, and he wanted to know how much I had kept track of what she did. In a business way."

"And you got out of it?"

"Out of what?"

Sader jammed the wheel in a circle, whirling the car into a side road, a dirt track that led between alfalfa fields to a row of packing sheds in the distance. There was no sign of life near them; there was just the imperishable green of the alfalfa, a smell of mowing, the sunlight, the whisper of the pepper trees behind them. Sader turned in the seat as the car rolled to a stop, gripped Kay's shoulders, pulled her close. She gasped as his lips closed over hers.

There was a welling of pressure, a pounding, in his head. He was rough, savage with her, because all that hatred, the despair worse than sickness, was suddenly directed against Kay, against her softness, her youth and fragrance. He tore at her lips as if he were tearing a net.

She tried to fight loose, and he sensed the scream bottled in her throat. He circled her neck with his arm, forcing her small head up so that their mouths still clung.

Time was a spiral, whirling down into disaster, an eternity of loathing for her and for himself; and inside that spiral, they were ageless, she was as old as he. Her sins had caught up with his years.

CHAPTER EIGHTEEN

At half past three they were climbing the grade of Cajon Pass, beyond San Bernardino. The air blowing in through the car windows had lost the smell of the city, of cultivated gardens. In it were odors of sun-baked earth and scrubby sage and the far-off dusty pockets of the desert. Ahead lay the long straight asphalt streak to Las Vegas.

Kay sat as far from Sader as she could get. She looked small and huddled in her corner. The hat had fallen off during their struggle earlier and she hadn't put it on again. Her bruised lips were puffed. She didn't talk.

Beyond Cajon Pass, feeling the warmth, Sader pulled into a roadside stand, bought Cokes, removed his outer coat. She took the Coke when he put it in through the window. She drank it without looking at Sader.

"It's going to be hot," he said. "Take off your jacket."

She didn't move, so he opened the door and pulled the jacket off her shoulders, down over her arms. She moved the bottled drink from one hand to the other; otherwise she might not have known what Sader was doing. He folded the little coat, put it on the back seat.

"I'm sorry I was rough with you."

She turned her head, not answering, not forgiving.

He said, "I'll tell you what I have planned. We'll go to Las Vegas, head north through Nevada, cut over and turn south and go into Mexico by way of El Paso. They'll be looking for us at Tijuana and Mexicali. I think we'll get by them as far east as El Paso."

"Why are you doing this?"

"I guess you know my reasons now."

"Please take me home, Mr. Sader." She sounded like a child.

"I can't. Pettis is wise by now. He'd have had some kind of watch on you. Some cop phoned in when you left with me. They know we headed out of town." He took the empty bottles back into the damply air-conditioned café, returned to the car, turned again into the highway.

Some miles further she said in a strangled voice, "You think I killed my mother!"

The sun was behind them. Its warmth lay in the car like the purring presence of some animal. Sader opened his shirt collar. "I don't care what you did. I don't even worry because you shot Dan. Not any more."

"I wouldn't do such things! I loved my mother. I thought Dan was one of the nicest people I'd ever met."

"What you thought of them didn't stand in your way."

"You must be crazy!"

"Skip it. I don't want to argue." Mostly, he thought, I don't want to have to run through it again, out loud, when I've tortured myself with it a hundred times since this trip began. All the reasons it had to be you—

Who could have impersonated Mrs. Wanderley well enough to clinch the later identification by the cab driver?

Whose guilt would have made Dan angry, as angry as he'd been on the phone, drumming words into Sader's ears that Sader didn't want to believe?

Who could have hurried home, smart enough to be there to answer a check up after Dan had been shot in the office?

Who had the motive?

Money could do a lot of things in this world. It could build you a castle, Sader told himself—or a dungeon. It could make you hungry for more. It could make you afraid of losing what you had, so that you were glad your wealthy mother no longer looked at men nor dallied with the idea of a second marriage. It could make you so suspicious that you killed when you found her alone with someone you took for a lover.

All of them straws, blowing in an inexorable wind. . . .

But the thing that completed it, tied it up tight, was Ajoukian's car in the garage of the vacant house. The car had been hidden by someone in a hell of a rush, Sader figured—someone who had to get it away before its presence called attention to the sump. The person who moved it had known precisely where to go.

As Kay would have known. . . .

He looked at the buff-colored landscape ahead, the flat empty valley through which the highway was drawn taut as wire, the fringes of rocky hills on the horizon, the shimmering mist of heat. It would be like this all the way into Las Vegas, excepting the brief oases of the little towns. He settled himself for the grind.

She asked finally, "When we get to Las Vegas may I call Annie?"

"Of course you can't. It would spoil everything."

"But she'll be worried!"

Sader shot her a frowning glance. "She won't even answer the phone. Pettis will pick up that receiver. He'll hear your voice, he'll trace the call, and where will you be?"

"I'm afraid of you," she cried. "I want to go home!"

"Afraid of me?" He laughed incredulously. "Don't you know what's waiting for you back there?" The car crested a long rise, dipped into another empty vista exactly like the one they'd left. The traffic, week-end gamblers coming back to L.A. after a fling in Las Vegas, began to thicken heavily. "I've got a friend in Las Vegas who'll cash a check for me," Sader mused, thinking out loud. "We're going to need money. I can leave him a power of attorney and he can sell my share of the business."

"Don't do that!"

"Why not?"

"This trip is meaningless, Mr. Sader. I didn't kill anyone. I don't have to run away! I'm sure Mr. Pettis has no suspicions of me."

"He's pretty cute that way," Sader put in.

"No, I'm convinced he believed in my innocence. Why should I kill my mother? She was moody and difficult, yes; she had a sickness of the mind. But we don't execute sick people."

"It was the money," Sader said firmly, out of his own belief.

"Mother's money? There was plenty for both of us. My father's will took care of me separately, anyway."

There was no place to draw off the road so Sader just rolled to a stop where he was, in the right lane of traffic, and let the honking cars dart around him. "You don't have to fool me, Kay. Get this straight. I'm not condemning you for what you did. Maybe you were a little crazy, too, from living with your boozy mother. She'd caused you to cut off all normal social life, to give up your friends, to live in dread of disgrace."

When he had pulled up, alarm flared in her face and she retreated into the corner, flattening herself on the door. "Please. . . ."

He kept his hands on the wheel. "I'm not going to touch you. I'll never touch you again unless you ask me to. Somewhere along the line we'd better get married, because of the legal aspects of the trip into Mexico. But you can call it a marriage of convenience. That's what it will be."

Her gray eyes were big, searching. After a minute she said, "Are you doing this because—because you think that you're in love with me?" There was sudden softness in her tone; and something that Sader thought, with a flare of dread, might almost be pity.

Pity was one thing he couldn't take. Deliberately he made his tone hard, amused. "Well, I hadn't quite figured it as—love."

Her face grew scarlet, she turned her head and the argument was over. She didn't look at him again. The hours ticked away on the clock on the dash; the miles fled under the tires. The sun began to draw far down in the west; there was coolness in the air and shadows lay long on the bare floor of the desert.

He turned on the car radio. Jazz bumped out, hot, compelling. If Kay heard it—and she could scarcely have helped this—she responded by not so much as the twitch of a muscle.

> . . . *He'll be big and strong*
> *The man I love* . . .

Sader punched a button, cutting off the sultry voice. There was news now. The news was about world-shaking things, armies marching, spies and secrets, elections, floods, famines. There was no mention of Long Beach, the town that had grown up from a village by the sea, a city with a hill in the middle of it, sprouting oil derricks like a forest of pins. There was no mention of murders, anywhere.

> . . . *He'll be big and strong*
> *The man I love* . . .

Crazy. He'd punched the same station back again. Sader clicked off the radio. Kay said quietly, "Didn't it occur to you that I might not want to marry you because there was somebody else?"

"Another man? No, I hadn't thought of it."

His clipped tone dismissed the subject. If Kay had had someone in love with her, he'd have been around during these last few days, during the search for her mother. Kay was trying to confuse him. She wanted to go back—funny kid—and get herself strapped into that chair in San Quentin's gas chamber.

The lights of a big roadside restaurant began to glow bright through the dusk ahead. Sader said, "I've got to have some coffee. How about some dinner for you?"

"I'm not hungry, thank you."

He pulled in under a neon archway to a graveled lot. This was Nevada. Through the big windows he could see a row of slot machines, some customers who couldn't wait for Las Vegas putting in dimes and quarters, pulling the levers to the thump of the jukebox wailing a torch tune.

He killed the motor, took the keys with him. Inside was a big half-finished barnlike room, half of it given over to the slots and a covered crap table, the other half a soda fountain and lunch counter. He stepped up, asked for a carton of coffee to take with him.

The kid behind the counter, eighteen or so, towheaded, wearing a white apron too big for him, shook his head. "Sorry. All out of them. Give you a clean can if it has to go. Would that do?"

"Sure."

The door opened behind Sader. There were three men at the other end of the counter and by the way they stared Sader knew that the newcomer must be Kay. The waiter, too, was eyeing the door. Sader turned around. She stood under the fan at the entry, and the stirring air caught her blond hair and twisted it. Sader hadn't realized how tired she looked until now. She came over to the counter and said to the waiter, "Do you have a telephone?"

"Yes, miss. Booth's back there." He pointed to the corner behind the crap table.

"I'll need some change." She handed the waiter a five dollar bill.

"Excuse me while I get her some change," the waiter said to Sader. The tone dismissed Sader's desire for coffee as being of little importance to this lovely girl's need for money with which to phone.

She walked to the booth. Sader followed her. She stepped into the cubicle, started to pull the door shut. Sader's foot was in the way. "Please go away, Mr. Sader."

"Give me a chance. Give me until Las Vegas. You can telephone Annie there, if you have to."

"If you don't take your foot out of the door, I'll complain to the clerk. He'll help me."

Yes, the towheaded kid would probably lay down his life, Sader thought. He'd die for stirring blond hair, for big gray eyes, for a figure as softly rounded as a ripe peach. Sader took his foot away. He went back to the counter. The waiter brought a tin can with coffee in it, newspaper-wrapped to hold the heat, to protect the hands. Sader paid for the coffee, went out to the car. It was growing dark now. There was a definite chill in the air. On the desert it was like that, he remembered. Hot days, cold nights. He propped the coffee on the seat, shrugged into his coat. Then he got in behind the wheel, sipped coffee, waited.

She ran out of the café and the fright in her reached him, all the way across the dark lot. It was something animal-like, primitive, about the way she held her head, too high, and the goad that plunged her toward the car. He turned the key in the switch, tossed the coffee out in one move. She fumbled at the door on the other side, then fell in, fell against Sader, hung there frozen.

He didn't try to drive. "What is it?"

"Annie."

He tried to push her back, to see her face. "What do you mean?"

"The police have been in my house. They think I'm guilty. Annie knows. She told me to keep on going."

It jarred. Sader couldn't say why—the advice was exactly what he'd been giving Kay all afternoon, indirectly—but having someone else tell this girl to run was like the stroke of a file against a nerve.

He felt other things in that moment, too. He was aware of the pain in his shoulder, where Ott had chopped him with the cleaver. The arm had ached all afternoon, but he'd ignored it, forced usefulness from the almost nerveless hand. Now the pain surged back, along with a dragging sense of being old and exhausted.

He seemed drowning in a terrible tide which lashed from him the last vestiges of youth. Kay's clinging arms, her young freshness, offered no foothold in that current. He'd been young once, yes; but that was over. It was really and finally over. The bitter truth was that he was now a tired man with gray in his hair, with the beginning of a stoop, and no amount of frenzy or cunning, no wishing, or of forcing his love upon the girl, could bring back that which had gone forever.

There must be a time like this in everyone's life, he

thought numbly. When all your illusions go down the drain. When you see at last what you have lost. When you reach out for someone like Kay and feel the barrier you never knew was there, the wall made of years.

He wanted to beat at something, to rip, to tear. Instead he pushed Kay gently away, closed the door behind her, reached for her jacket on the back seat, and fixed it across her shoulders. "You didn't kill them."

"No," she whispered.

"Don't be afraid, then. We'll go into Las Vegas—it isn't far now. I'll do some telephoning. We'll decide what to do."

Her voice shook with the effort to control her fear. "I don't want to go to Mexico."

"We aren't going to Mexico. I guess we never were. Funny." He started the motor; the car crept out toward the road. The lights ahead were like a string of fireflies in the night. In less than an hour they should see the glow from Las Vegas. "Try to get some sleep."

"No, I want to talk. Why were you so sure I'd murdered Mother?"

"For several reasons." Leaning on the wheel, he rubbed the side of his head. The lights dazzled his eyes, there was a headache through his temples. "It seemed to stack up. The cab driver must by now have identified your mother as the woman he took out to Veterans' Hospital Wednesday morning. If he hadn't, if there was a question of imposture, it should have come out. It hasn't. And yet, the way I figure, your mother was dead that Wednesday morning at five o'clock."

"Do you think I resemble her *that* much?"

"I was surprised," Sader said. He wished he'd drunk all the coffee, or had some aspirin with him.

"What was the purpose of all this?"

"Oh, I think the trip in the cab was supposed to draw attention from the Hill, from that sump. Just as hiding young Ajoukian's car was meant to do."

"What about the coat?"

"Thrown in later. The next night, perhaps." He forced himself away from the wheel, tried to sit straight, think straight. "Of course, if the plan had succeeded, if your mother and young Ajoukian hadn't been discovered for weeks—"

She was silent, hating, he knew, the picture conjured up by his words.

"Wait—" Catching the fugitive idea that haunted him was like chasing a goldfish. It darted, slithered away, and he was distracted by the flashing lights that stung his eyes, then poured on into the dark. "If the murderer's plan had worked, the identification by the cab driver wouldn't have meant anything. All he really remembered was a fur coat, a scarf, a woman who gave her name in the process of raising hell so he'd remember her. Without a corpse in good condition—"

"Please—"

He drove on in silence, exploring the possibilities. The killer couldn't have expected young Ajoukian and Mrs. Wanderley to be found so quickly. If the bodies had remained hidden, if their fate had been merely a matter for speculation—

He let the picture fill itself in.

226

Among the people who knew these two, there would have been gradual changes. Those who loved them would have faced a slow encroachment of despair. Those to whom their absence meant advantage would have gradually moved more into the open.

With Felicia Wanderley gone, old Ajoukian's purchase of the oil shares would have proceeded without notice. Ott would have received his cut. Ott's duplex could admittedly have been sold and off the market. Milton would have had relief from her tirades about the pigs.

What about young Ajoukian?

Sader thought to himself that the situation might be complicated by factors of which he knew nothing; but from present knowledge Ajoukian, Jr.'s absence seemed to benefit nobody. His father had been frantic with worry —up until Sader's final visit, when the old man was consoling himself with the thought that his bright boy could look after himself. The young widow had appeared at all times normally anxious, though finally not overcome with grief. Many people suffered deeply from loss without visible sign, and she could be one of them. Be fair to her, Sader reminded himself. It's not everyone has to live with a cantankerous mummy, and a gorilla.

The appellation reminded Sader of something Dan had said at the beginning, that young Ajoukian was the type who might like to leap on women out of dark corners just for kicks. Dan had sized him up as having a brutal streak. Put that idea alongside the facts about Mrs. Wanderley, her violent and drunken mood on Tuesday night.

The only wonder was that they hadn't killed *each other*.

CHAPTER NINETEEN

Kay was watching him from her corner. "What are you thinking about?"

"Young Ajoukian." He took out cigarettes, offered Kay one, lit both with the lighter from the dash. "Dan worked on that angle. He has information I need." The first call from Las Vegas, he told himself, would be to the hospital.

"If his car had been hidden where you say it was, in that house Mother had listed to sell, it could mean simply that the murderer was familiar with the neighborhood."

"Yes, that must be it."

She went on, her tone very serious. "If the murderer posed as Mother to the cab driver, it—"

"Wait a minute," Sader interrupted. "Let's don't jump to *that* conclusion. The murderer may have had a friend. The friend may possibly have carried through the impersonation without realizing its import."

"That's asking a lot of friendship," she protested. "I wouldn't do a thing like that unless I knew its purpose."

"Suppose the murderer had a hold over the woman—"

"You mean, you think the murderer is a man?"

"I haven't any evidence, one way or another. I don't think your mother and young Ajoukian stood precisely on the rim of that sump to argue about the sale of Mrs. Cole's oil shares. Nearby—perhaps. It would have taken some strength to have dragged them up that embankment and pitched them in."

"Mother was slender, almost frail."

Sader turned briefly to glance at her, to rest his eyes from the spinning lights. She'd tucked her legs under her. The soft green silk was drawn tight across her slender knees. Above the deep V of her blouse, her throat had a creamy pallor. Sader said, "Ajoukian was young, well-built, husky. Six foot tall at least, judging by what I saw of him stretched on the embankment. Well-muscled shoulders. A bear of a fellow." With a shock, Sader realized that his tone had been etched with envy.

"If you thought *I* killed him, and Mother, then you must have believed I could have tugged him up that bank, somehow."

"It would have taken time."

"But it wouldn't have been impossible."

"No, I guess it wouldn't."

The glow from Las Vegas' Strip, the long arm of luxury casinos and hotels that reached out toward the migrating suckers from L.A., began to light up the sky ahead. Soon the car raced between neon-lit palaces, the Sands, Sahara, Flamingo, Last Frontier. Ahead was the whiter conflagration of the downtown district. Sader pulled into a service station, left the car by the pumps to be filled, went over to the telephone booth beside the station door. Kay followed him, as he previously had followed her. He left the door open, however. She stood listening while he put through the call to the hospital.

This was another nurse, softer-voiced, more co-operative. She said, "Yes, Mr. Sader—Mr. Scarborough did become conscious, though briefly. He's resting easily now. He's still in danger, of course, but Dr. Heffelmaier seems to think he'll pull through."

"That's wonderful!" Sader was aware of sudden warm gratitude toward these people, unknown to him or to Dan, who'd given time and skill to saving Dan's life. "I was wondering, though—did he say anything?"

"Dr. Heffelmaier seemed to think that what he said may have been meant for you. Considering the circumstances, you know."

"And what was it?" Sader asked, burning with impatience.

"The little we are sure of is quite brief." She seemed to be apologizing. "Mostly, Mr. Scarborough spoke incoherently. At one point his voice took on definite emphasis. He said, 'I'm telling you—it's the week. . . .'"

"The week?" Sader repeated.

"I took it to mean a length of time. Though there's another meaning. And he added the words, *slim ankles*, a little later."

"That was all?"

"I'm sorry. Yes."

"Is anyone keeping a watch over him?" Sader asked suddenly. "I mean, in case of another attack—"

"There is a police officer at his door," she said.

"Thank you."

"You're welcome, Mr. Sader."

He stepped from the booth, lit a cigarette for Kay, for himself, tried to think it through. Over by the pumps, the car was getting its windshield cleaned, its oil checked. The traffic headed westward was a steadily thickening stream.

"What will you do now?" Kay wondered.

"Go back," Sader told her.

"Have you found out something?"

"Yes, I guess so." He took a long look at the glow of Las Vegas, the pool of light that dimmed the stars overhead. He'd had some crazy plans back there, he thought. Marrying Kay, taking her to Mexico. On what?

He turned his back on the town, on what it might have meant to him and now never could, and touched Kay's elbow, guiding her to the car.

He left Kay in the rear booth of an all-night café on Atlantic. "Order something to eat. Take your time over it. In about an hour, go home in a cab. I'll have it whipped by then—or never."

Her gaze on Sader was calm, confident. You had to look close to see any sign of her being up all night. There were fine lines drawn around her eyes, but they'd be gone after an hour or so of sleep. To Sader the bitter grainy itch of exhaustion seemed ground into his bones. Age, Papa, he thought, talking to himself in Dan's voice. You're getting old. He felt her hand, touching his softly. "Come to my house later," she was saying.

Sader nodded. He took another long look at the uplifted face, the curve of the chin he'd memorized, the gray eyes to haunt his dreams. "Good-bye." He walked out of the café. He knew he'd never see her again.

There was a burst of green light on the eastern horizon and against it the outline of the Hill, its forest of rigs, was like that of a sleeping porcupine. Sader pulled himself into his car, started the motor, turned south to Seventh Street. He drove out Seventh, not too fast, hating now the errand he was on. He left Long Beach behind, came to open country, then to the neatly landscaped scraps of acreage where people bored with city life played at being farmers. The air was very fragrant out here. Someone had cut hay, and there was wood smoke on the breeze, some early riser—or somebody who hadn't got around to going to bed—warming himself at a hearth, and in the distance a lot of roosters were crowing.

The Ajoukian lane was shadowy, the house unlit. Sader parked the car and walked over to ring the doorbell, and to wait. The nurse came finally, pinning her cap. She was a new nurse, since the old man had a sharp turnover in his help. She was small, stout, red-headed, and somehow made Sader think of a Peke. He said, "I'd like to see Mrs. Ajoukian."

"At this hour?" Her voice was yappy, like a Peke's, and her snub nose wriggled in suspicion. "My God, nobody's up."

"Well, you're up. Tell her it's Sader to see her."

"Who are you? I mean, are you a relative, or someone

close to the family? I'm asking on account of the old man. He's very low."

"You're a girl after my own heart," Sader complimented her, "and the first nurse I've ever met who actually passed out information about the patient. How long has he got?"

"Not very long." She took the last of the pins out of her mouth, so she could talk plainly. Her voice got deeper, so some of the Peke impression vanished. "He's had a stroke."

"Can he talk?"

"A little. He's not unconscious, just confused. He thinks he's back in the past somewhere, raising hell about grocery bills. Then he cries some about a little girl dying." She patted her hair around the rim of the starched cap, opened the door a little wider. "Shall I see if Mrs. Ajoukian wants to see you at this hour?"

"It was the general idea," Sader commented. She left the door ajar, so Sader could look in at the hall, the glass brick, the tumbled greenery in the brick planters. He felt the dawn growing behind his back, a gray flood stealing up the sky. He wanted to sleep. He didn't like to have to think about old Ajoukian, grieving for the daughter dead all these years.

When young Mrs. Ajoukian appeared, she was wearing a blue silk housecoat. For somebody who'd just been wakened, she seemed quite alert. She looked at Sader through the door and said, "Is it something important?"

"It's about Dan."

She stepped back, and he went in. The nurse said something about making coffee for all of them, and disappeared.

233

They faced each other there in the hall, with the wet smell from the planters filling the air, and somewhere outside a rooster crowing his head off. Sader thought that Mrs. Ajoukian knew at once what he'd come about. She was a woman of remarkable composure. Finally she asked, "Is your partner dead yet?"

"No. It seems he might not be going to die."

"Has he talked to you?"

"A little."

She nodded as if this confirmed some unspoken surmise. "Do you happen to have a cigarette?"

"Sure." He offered his pack, she picked one out, he lit it for her. She smoked for a minute, thoughtfully, her eyes not on Sader's face but on some point just past his shoulder. The loose pale hair shone under the hall lights. The curls on her shoulders, Sader thought, looked exactly like the spun-sugar candy they sold on the Pike.

"Why have you come here?" she asked. "Why not go to the police?"

"You were our client," Sader answered. "It's considered very bad for business to turn clients over to the cops."

"But you're fond of your partner, aren't you?"

"He can be an aggravating guy."

She shook her head. "No, that's not it. You're hoping I'll make a break, try to run, give myself away. I might add that I called on Pettis late last night, just checking up on the progress of the case you understand, and he seemed awfully eager to know where you were. You and that Miss Wanderley."

"There's nothing you can do at this stage of the game," Sader told her. "If you want to try to get away, I'll hold off. They'll be coming here eventually. You might have an hour or two."

"Aren't they going to arrest Miss Wanderley?"

"I don't think so."

"Before they can charge me with murder," she said rapidly, "they'll have to figure out a motive. What did I gain? They'll have to build a case—how I planned it all—"

"You didn't," Sader interrupted. "You followed your husband that night out of jealousy. Because he was hell on wheels with the girls. Because he was beginning to listen to his old man, to think that with all that money he was a fool to be tied down to you. His date in the bar didn't come off. You probably peeped in now and then, saw him sitting alone. Perhaps you figured he was wise to you, was playing it smart. When it was around eleven he had a telephone call. It was Mrs. Wanderley, but you had no way of knowing that. The old man wanted Perry to meet her, to shut her up before she spoiled the deal to buy Mrs. Cole's property."

"You *are* a faker," she murmured.

"I'm just figuring. You trailed Perry to the Hill, where he met Mrs. Wanderley. The woman was drunk and violent, and he was trying to quiet her down. To you, in your mood, it looked like passion."

"Okay." She nodded in irony. "What did I shoot them with?"

"Not with Mrs. Wanderley's gun. It wasn't loaded. You took it away with you, afterward, to confuse the picture.

You took her coat, too, and remembering her hair done in a scarf, you got yourself up in similar garb to stage the scene with the cab driver."

She laughed, richly, throatily, and under the lights her beauty seemed to blaze in triumph. She was gorgeous; he was never more conscious of it than at that moment, nor more conscious, too, of how cold her beauty left him.

"Meanwhile, you'd driven Perry's car away, stumbled on a house for sale where the garage was empty—"

For the first time there was a crack, a split, in the brittle composure. For just an instant fright flickered in her eyes. It had to do with that house. Sader backtracked slowly. "Wait a minute. I see a possibility. You weren't happy here under the thumb of old Ajoukian. You looked around for a place, hoping to coax your husband to move into it with you, to live alone where the old man couldn't poison him against you. Close to the Hill, where he had business contacts. There might even be someone who remembers your looking at the place, some neighbor—"

The fright was naked, open, now. She licked her lips. She was like some lovely and poisonous flower getting ready to explode with venom.

"You still haven't proved–the gun—" She tried to sneer again, but now her mouth was shaking.

"I guess I don't know which gun—" Sader stopped talking. Behind her the inner door had opened and old Ajoukian stood there tottering. It wasn't the sight of the crippled, emaciated figure that stunned Sader; it was what the old man held in his hand. A gun as bright, deadly, venomous, as the girl herself. "No–wait!"

"Why should I?" came the cracked, cackling voice. The girl started, color draining from her face; but she didn't turn around to face her father-in-law. The old man went on, "I tried to make them hold her. I cooked up something, I thought if they got her in jail they'd get the truth out of her. Perry gone, in trouble maybe like Mullens thought—her fault. Now I know it all. The dirt she did my boy." His hand rose, wobbled, and Sader dived for the floor.

The sound of the shot filled the passage. The greenery seemed to bend under the report, and there was a popping noise from one of the glass bricks. For a minute Sader thought she'd gotten off without hurt. She looked at old Ajoukian. "You old devil. . . ." But now there was a seeping stain on her arm.

The old man fired again. And again. Then he leaned in the doorway and began to cry, a high grinding screech like an injured parrot's. "This gun. This gun she used. Mine. To kill my son." The cries went on and on, drowning the screams of the nurse who had come to look, then fled.

Sader crawled over to where she lay. Her eyes were open, though they were glazing. Sader didn't think she saw him, that her words were meant for him. "I really didn't dream she was that old." He knew she meant Mrs. Wanderley. "She really was a good-looking woman." It was a kind of apology to Perry for the natural mistake, Sader thought. Addressed to Perry, whom she ought to be seeing again before too long.

There was one last whisper. "I didn't like that part—putting them in the oil."

Well, Perry had been a very handsome man, and putting him in the sump had been cruel to those good looks. She was a girl whose regrets would concern surface things, appearances, bodily decencies. She wouldn't worry whether Perry, in those last few moments, had had time to repent the amours of an overfull existence. She'd worry about the oil, eating out his eyes . . .

The old man still had the gun, and there was no guarantee he wouldn't use it again. Sader went out through the front door, around the rear to the garden shut in by ivy walls. The nurse was there. She was being sick into a bed of begonias.

"Excuse me. I'm easily upset." She staggered wretchedly to a bench.

Sader said, "Is there a telephone in the kitchen?"

"You'd go in *there*!" she screamed.

"He's pointed the other way." Sader went into the kitchen, found the phone hidden behind a copper screen in the barbecue area, called Pettis. There wasn't much to tell.

When he was through with the phone, Sader sat down on a bench by the barbecue table to wait. The house was silent. The beautiful, expensive house was as still as a tomb.

CHAPTER TWENTY

Pettis was mad. He had a foot on the redwood bench, his cigar dribbled ashes on the barbecue table. "The cab driver *didn't* identify Mrs. Wanderley positively as the woman he saw Wednesday morning. He said he hadn't had a particularly good look at her face, with her busy kicking his shins and so on. One thing he was pretty positive about—the slacks were the wrong color. The woman in his cab had dark green slacks, almost black. Mrs. Wanderley's, even stained with oil, were a brighter blue-green. I was getting ready to give him a look at the other women in the case when you took off with Miss Wanderley. What was I supposed to think?"

"Yeah, yeah." Sader tried to rub the sand out of his eyes. "I just wish once you boys had rushed things a little. If you'd taken Mrs. Ajoukian in on suspicion she'd be alive now."

"Alive for what?"

"Oh, time to think anyhow. To repent, perhaps. I don't think she would have gotten the gas chamber. She was a gorgeous hunk of gal and her husband was beginning to neglect her. He'd been listening to his old man's ideas, love 'em and leave 'em."

"Well, give me the meat of it. What started you after her?"

"I wish I could say it was Mullens's murder. That should have done it. Mullens had contacted old man Ajoukian, hinting his son was in trouble and had had to hide the car. I don't know what had happened. Something seemed to make Mullens think of drunk driving. At least, it's what he mentioned to me."

"The car has a bent fender," Pettis put in. "We didn't have any report from another car, anyone being hit, so my guess is in the excitement she ran it into an embankment."

Sader nodded. It fitted into the pattern. "Mullens must have thought that the car's being hidden as it was meant something pretty embarrassing had happened. He glimpsed a woman in a fur coat and slacks, probably from a distance and at night, waited until the coast was clear and got the name and address off the car in the garage, thought it over, finally put the bee on old Ajoukian for a few thousand. Being on the Hill and in the oil game, he'd know the son's reputation. The old man was too tightfisted to pay off right away, but he was plenty upset. Remember, it was the next day that he tried to kick me off the case. This was before he knew Mullens had been murdered."

"You said that Mullens's murder should have sent you after the girl. Why?"

"I knew yesterday that Mullens had been in touch with old Ajoukian. I should have remembered how scared

Mullens got when he heard that a woman was missing. Mullens thought it over, began not to like the possibilities. It was only natural that after my visit he'd contact old Ajoukian again. But by then the old man was in a collapse with worry, and Mrs. Ajoukian would naturally take the call. Mullens let something slip, enough to let her see her danger. My guess is, he said to tell old Mr. Ajoukian their deal was off and he was going to the cops. That sump would almost surely have been investigated."

"She made quick work of him," Pettis growled. "But since all this didn't flash through your mastermind, what did make you think of her?"

"Well, finally, it was what Dan said at the hospital."

Obviously Pettis had heard of it long before Sader had. He'd picked those few words thoroughly apart. "Something about a week. And ankles, of all damn items."

"No, you've got to put the two together. *Weak ankles.* Mrs. Ajoukian suffered from them, she was always turning her ankles on something. I noticed it, the few times we were together. Dan would have. He must have been staring at her legs right along."

"So?" Pettis went to the sink, discarded the cigar there. "So what?"

"The vine." Sader rubbed the muscles at the back of his neck, under his collar. They were tight as wire. "The torn vine, beside the office door. Someone fell into it about the time Mullens was murdered. Maybe a witness. Maybe someone peeping in at the door, as you thought."

Pettis grinned briefly. Perhaps he was remembering his trick on Tina Griffin at the office.

"Or again," Sader went on, "maybe the murderer fell there. I kept thinking of someone fat and awkward like Charlie Ott. But then I remembered that when you and Dan and I were having the late interview in the office, Dan sat facing the door, the dark. Someone was out there. I heard a footstep and was surprised that no one entered. My guess is it was Mrs. Ajoukian, just checking up generally, listening to what she could hear. Dan smiled at one point as if recognizing someone. He must have caught a glimpse of her, perhaps of that pale hair that always caught the light. But a minute later he looked grim. My guess—he saw the edge of the fallen vine. It occurred to him in that instant that Mrs. Ajoukian was the logical one to have stumbled there, turning an ankle in her hurry to get away from the man she had just murdered."

Pettis swore. "Oh, such rot! It doesn't mean a damned thing! Nobody ever got convicted on such flimsy stuff!"

"You're so right. That's why Dan kept his mouth shut to you about it. Probably he didn't even mention it to Mrs. Ajoukian when she answered his call to come to the office. Remember the papers he had spread out, my notes about the interview with the Ajoukians? He was running a bluff, pretending to have found something in my report which had developed a lead to her."

Pettis's eyes had grown speculative, thoughtful. "Yes, it could be."

"It's the only explanation that fits. The papers were there for some reason, though we could never figure why. They were a fake, a trap. She must have arrived full of confidence that she could argue Dan out of his silly obsession. In case she couldn't she had Mr. Ajoukian's gun along."

"She knew how to use it."

"Plenty of practice by then. I still can't figure how he's alive, even going to live. I guess the first part of the interview between them wasn't too unpleasant. Dan was thoroughly smitten with her and she'd have had to be blind not to notice. She probably tried her wiles on him. He got mad though. Dan's nerves were popping these last few days. While she was there he went all the way with the bluff, calling me to rave about what fools she'd made of us. Mostly he must have been mad because a beautiful gal had made such a sucker out of him."

"Oh, hell, women are doing it all the time," Pettis growled.

Dan opened his eyes and said huskily, "Hi there, Papa. I thought you were in Las Vegas."

"It was just a rumor. Where'd you hear it?"

"I can't imagine," Dan whispered. "Someone must have told me in my sleep. How's Mrs. Ajoukian?"

"She's all right."

"Don't let them hurt her, Papa."

"Do you want her to have years and years in prison?"

Dan began to act agitated. The nurse came forward, frowning. Sader said, "All right, all right. I won't rile him."

She went back to her chair by the window.

Dan began to breathe evenly again. "I guess you and the Wanderley babe are hitting it off, huh?"

"Oh, sure. I'm adopting her next week. She's an orphan now, needs a father."

Dan's breathy whisper protested, "Don't try to fool me. Lots of old boys marrying young babes lately."

"Those particular old boys had a few items like money and reputation lying around."

Belligerently Dan tried to sit up. The nurse came tearing over with fire in her eye. Dan went on yelling while she tried to press his shoulders back to the pillow.

At the door, Sader thought, he's going to be all right. Then he left. Going down in the hospital elevator, Sader felt worry slip from him. The suddenly relaxed feeling made him almost dizzy. He rubbed the close-cropped hair, grinning at the elevator girl, then threw back his head and walked out of the hospital entry in a glow of warmth. This was something to celebrate!

He was too keyed up to go home. He drove downtown, parked the car, went up to his office. He'd snatch an hour's nap on the couch, then go out to a café for lunch, then feel like a million all over. The fuzziness behind his eyes would be gone, the bubbling excitement about Dan would die down. Maybe the terrible heavy feeling inside somewhere would go away, too.

There were some pretty quick remedies available, of course. He tried to force from his thoughts the image of Dan's bottle, but it stayed as if caught in some cobweb in a corner of his mind. The tantalizing rum . . .

Whiskey was better, but of course he'd learned long ago he couldn't drink, not anything. He let himself into the office, shed the coat, looked blankly at his and Dan's desks. What had he come here for?

There was a step in the outer room. Sader swung

around. There was a sort of cloud in front of his eyes, and he couldn't breathe. The light steps came close to the door. The door swung open.

He saw the check in her hand through the quivering light, so it had to be Kay—she'd come to pay him. An excuse. He said hoarsely, "You didn't have to do that."

"She wanted you to have it," said Tina Griffin. It was Tina Griffin's voice, so he took a quick look at the face. And that was Tina's too, a lovely face with exotic eyes. Very white skin, like the petals of a white camellia. Black hair as fine as silk. "I was at her house when she got home. That Annie character was boarding up the windows, practically, getting ready to stave off a siege by the police. It took a little straightening out. Then Kay said, she owed you so much. And she sent this. A thousand dollars, for finding her mother."

Sader took the check and shredded it all over the top of the two desks like a cloud of confetti.

Tina Griffin sat down in a chair, then noticed the couch, moved over there. "I thought you'd do that, so I had Kay make out another, a second check, just in case. It's made out to your partner, and I'll keep it in my purse until I can give it to him."

Sader leaned on the desk, looking at her. "That was very clever of you."

"Not so clever. Kay told me about the trip to Las Vegas." She was getting a cigarette from her handbag. Sader took out matches, lit it for her, still watching her angrily. "Kay has so much money. She won't miss the thousand. She's going away."

"Going—"

"Just a trip. Hawaii, or somewhere." The exotic eyes on his had no pity in them, Sader saw; and for this he was relieved. She was explaining something to him, very matter of fact, so he'd understand why his client might not have time for a final interview.

"I never intended to try to see her again."

"I guessed that, too."

He walked around, looking at the furniture. Dan had bought it, picked it out, saying that he was determined it shouldn't look like a private eye's office. That's exactly what it looked like, of course. Every TV studio, every movie lot, had its duplicate, always used by private detectives for interviewing clients.

Or for fighting villains who'd come to raid the safe.

Or for drinking . . .

He took out Dan's bottle, put it on the desk, went to the outer room and came back with a couple of paper cups.

She leaned forward, amused. "What are you doing?"

Sader smiled tightly. "I, too, am going on a trip."

"Are you, really? Or are you trying to get rid of me?" She got up from the couch and came over to the desk. "I was hoping you'd be around. I like you very much," she added, on a note of shyness that Sader thought intriguing.

He gave her a paper cup with rum in it. "Need a chaser?"

She shook her head, her eyes on his over the rim of the cup. "No, thanks."

She was a very good-looking woman, Sader thought. He remembered the scene in Mullens's office—she'd hoped to meet him again when he wasn't working. It occurred to

Sader that this was it. He was fresh out of jobs. He put an arm around her slender waist. She was supple and yielding, her hair satiny against his cheek, her perfume mixing itself with the warmer, rather medicinal odor of the rum.

Sader touched his cup to hers. "Here's to high diving," he said.

ABOUT DOLORES HITCHENS AND STEPH CHA

In a 1952 letter to her editor at Doubleday, Dolores Hitchens wryly explained that her full name, thanks to "a series of step-fathers and two husbands," was "Julia Clara Catherine Maria Dolores Robins Norton Birk Olsen Hitchens." She was born in San Antonio, Texas, on December 25, 1907, her parents W. H. Robbins and Myrtle (Statham) Robbins "of pioneer Texas stock." She later remembered her great-great-grandmother as "the first woman to step on Texas soil with Austin's colony," and her grandfather as "a sheriff during the wild-and-woolly period." She spent her grammar school years in the "oil-field country" of Kern County, California, her father dying while she was an infant and her mother subsequently divorcing a second husband. In 1922, the family moved to Long Beach, California, where her mother married Oscar Carl Birk and where Julia Birk (as Hitchens was then called) went to high school. Her literary career began during her high school years, with the publication of stories and poems in *The Long Beach Press* and the sale of a short poem to *Motion Picture Magazine*, where it appeared in July 1924.

After graduation, now calling herself Dolores Birk, Hitchens attended UCLA and worked in nearby Seal Beach for two years as a third-grade teacher. On August 3, 1931, at twenty-three, she married Beverley S. Olsen, a ship's purser and radio operator, in San Francisco; they moved in with her parents, and on July 5, 1935, had a daughter, Patricia Marie. Three years later, as D. B. Olsen, Hitchens published her first novel, *The Clue in the Clay*; the following year, in 1939, she published a second novel featuring its detective protagonist Lieutenant Stephen Mayhew, *Death Cuts a Silhouette*, and then *Cat Saw Murder*, the first novel in what would become her popular, twelve-novel series of "cat" mysteries centered around spinster-detective Rachel Murdock.

Hitchens divorced Olsen to marry Hubert A. Hitchens, an investigator for the Southern Pacific Railroad Police and the father of two teenage sons, in late 1940 or 1941. On July 18, 1942, they had a son of their own, Michael John. She enjoyed "cooking elaborate dishes, dabbling in sculpture, raising fancy chickens, and traveling in a 'jalopy,'" according to a biographical sketch published in 1943. She took psychology courses at a local college, "with the ultimate aim of outfitting my characters with the latest in psychoses and fixations." The new family lived in and around Long Beach for the next sixteen years, with some time spent in the Northern California town of Eureka in the late 1940s. Her daughter Patricia married in 1952. In 1955, with her husband and son, she vacationed in Havana.

While she continued to write novels and magazine stories under her nom de plume D. B. Olsen—including a six-volume series of mysteries featuring English literature professor A. Pennyfeather, and a 1962 western, *The Night of the Bowstring*—her new name gave Hitchens "a fresh lease on life" and "a new reincarnation, book-wise." Moving away from D. B. Olsen's cozier, more domestic style, the novels of Dolores Hitchens—including *Stairway to an Empty Room* (1951), *Nets to Catch the Wind* (1952), *Terror Lurks in Darkness* (1953), *Beat Back the Tide* (1954), the James Sader mysteries *Sleep with Strangers* (1955) and *Sleep with Slander* (1960), and *Fool's Gold* (1958), the last adapted by French New Wave director Jean-Luc Godard for his 1964 film *Bande à part* (*Band of Outsiders*)—are increasingly suspenseful and hard-boiled thrillers. She also wrote novels under the pseudonyms Dolan Birkley and Noel Burke, and she collaborated with Bert Hitchens on an innovative series of railroad police procedurals that included *F.O.B. Murder* (1955), *One-Way Ticket* (1956), *End of the Line* (1957), *The Man Who Followed Women* (1959), and *The Grudge* (1963).

Divorcing her husband in 1959, Hitchens moved to an apartment in nearby Anaheim. Her later Dolores Hitchens novels include *The Watcher* (1959), *Footsteps in the Night* (1961), *The Abductor* (1962), *The Bank with the Bamboo Door* (1965), *The Man Who Cried All the Way Home* (1966), *Postscript to Nightmare* (1967), *A Collection of Strangers* (1969), *The Baxter Letters* (1971), and *In a House Unknown* (1973). She died at sixty-five on August 1, 1973, and was buried in Holy Sepulcher Cemetery in Orange, California.

*

Steph Cha is the author of *Your House Will Pay*, winner of the *Los Angeles Times* Book Prize and the California Book Award, and the Juniper Song crime trilogy. She's a critic whose work has appeared in the *Los Angeles Times*, *USA Today*, and the *Los Angeles Review of Books*, where she served as noir editor, and is the current series editor of the *Best American Mystery & Suspense* anthology. A native of the San Fernando Valley, she lives in Los Angeles with her family.